Follow Me

First Story

Carriage House Chronicles

Kelly Kay

Follow Me
Copyright @2023 by Kelly Kay/Kelly Kreglow
All rights reserved
Visit my website www.kellykayromance.com

Cover Design: Dena Light
Editor: Aimee Walker : Aimee Walker Editorial Services
www.aimeewalkerproofreader.com

This work originally appeared in the anthology A Series of Unfortunate
Meet Cutes.

This is a work of fiction. Names, characters, places, and incidents are
either a product of the author's imagination, public domain and any
resemblance to actual persons, living or dead, business establishments,
events or locales are coincidental, or if an actual place or person, they are
used fictitiously.

The author acknowledges the trademarked status of various products
referenced in this work of fiction, which have been used without
permission. The use of these trademarks is not sponsored, associated, or
endorsed by the trademark owner.

Published by Decorated Cast Publishing, LLC

❀ Created with Vellum

How The Chronicles Work
Welcome to the Carriage House Chronicles.

They're a series of novellas set in a Chicago carriage house that are low commitment, highly entertaining, no cliffhanger, and happily ever afters.

I created them to be consumed in an afternoon, a long morning or an evening. They're what you read when you don't know what to read next.

I'm randomly releasing them when I finish them throughout the year. You can pre-order, but know that date isn't when they'll be released. I'm going to publish them as soon as they're ready. They'll just appear on your Kindle like a surprise present.

There are four of them planned, including a December holiday one.

At least one main character in each of them will come from the Lyrical Duet: *Shock Mount & Crossfade.* I'll refer to those books, but you don't have to have read them to enjoy these stories.

Hope you enjoy!

But if you want to read them, they're on Amazon and in Kindle Unlimited for now! You can start Shock Mount by clicking on the words Shock Mount (Unless you have a paperback and in that case, you'll have to do a little bit more work.)

Quick Note

Follow Me is a spoiler for ***Shock Mount and Crossfade*** as it very specifically takes place after both of those books. Main plot points are revealed pretty quickly.

If you don't care - then dive right in. But it is NOT necessary to read them to enjoy this story. It is a complete standalone story.

If you want to read that duet, it's currently in Kindle Unlimited and available on Amazon. Click below if you want to.

Other than being trapped in tight spaces, there are no triggers.

Thanks!!

Enjoy

Kelly K

Also by Kelly Kay

FIVE FAMILIES VINEYARD ROMANCES

LaChappelle/Whittier Vineyard Trilogy

Crushing, Rootstock & Uncorked

Stafýlia Cellars Duet

Over A Barrel & Under The Bus

Gelbert Family Winery

Meritage: An Unexpected Blend

Residual Sugar

STILL TO COME

Pietro Family (Pre-Order is live)

It's time to tell the whole story of a different kind of family.

Langerford Cellars

* * * *

CROSSTOWN BOSTON CREW: A SECOND CHANCE SERIES

Keep Paris

Keep Philly - a newsletter exclusive novelette April 2023

Keep Vegas - Summer 2023 - Pre-order is live

* * * *

CHI TOWN ROMANCES

A Lyrical Romance Duet

Shock Mount & Crossfade

A Lyrical Spinoff Standalone

Present Tense

* * * *

STANDALONE

Side Piece: A workaholic romance

* * * *

EVIE & KELLY'S HOLIDAY DISASTERS

ROMCOM Holiday Novellas with Evie Alexander

VOLUME ONE

Cupid Calamity

Cookout Carnage

Christmas Chaos

* * * *

CARRIAGE HOUSE CHRONICLES

Funny, steamy, smart novellas for when you don't know what to read next. Released randomly throughout the year! Like a surprise for your Kindle.

Follow Me - Now available

Sound Off

Something Good

(This will first appear in Twisted Tropes Anthology available
March 30 and join the Chronicles in the fall)

For the Rest of Us

Reading orders, playlists and book info can all be found at www.
kellykayromance.com

For Allison, Cindy & Celia the original members of the Ian Reilly fan club.

Chapter 1
Ingrid

"Ingrid. Ingrid. Here. Look here!!"

Flashes pop, but it's daylight, so it doesn't bother me. However, the dude walking backward and recording is annoying.

"Mademoiselle Schroeder! Ingrid Schroeder. Rumor has it Dior fired you." Fuck. I can't even quit a job without judgment. Do they think I can't speak French after three years in this country? Why yell at me in English? "Représentez-vous Dior?" A pointed man says. I ignore him.

No, asshole, I don't rep Dior. Like I've been based out of Paris simply for free clothes. I fucking work there, and I worked my ass off for the respect I've earned through the company, not because of how many followers I can show off to.

I shield my mouth and talk into my phone. They have literally lip-read conversations before. People feel like I abandoned my 522k Instagram followers. But what were they following anyway? I hate this.

"Dad, there's paps. I haven't been an influencer for three years. Why can't they leave me alone?"

"The more you don't want attention, the more they want you, Little Bell."

I turn to my stalkers. "Translate this: Your family must be so proud. Taking a picture of a girl walking to lunch. You're the bee's knees." I scowl and push through.

"They asked if Dior was a glamour job. I was super successful and quit on my own terms, but they think I was fired." I glare at the man who asked if I repped Dior. No. I fucking bought this dress.

"Little Bell. Focus on my voice and your goodbye speech you're giving for your luncheon. Walk away." Always my father's advice.

"There's no second act for an influencer and party celebs. Kim, the Grande dame can't even have legitimate businesses without everyone thinking someone else is doing the work for her."

"Have your farewell lunch so you can hurry home to Sonoma. I'll have pancakes waiting."

I smile, and the cameras go nuts as I yank open the door. I'm early. I don't love talking to groups, now. I'm freaking out about it because, inevitably, someone will film it and post it. I know it makes no sense for someone who's been photographed as often as I have to be nervous. But that's all a machine that feeds itself. I'm literally famous for nothing.

I fell in with Gigi and Bella because we loved fashion. They made me laugh, and I trust them to this day. I didn't give a shit about who their parents were or what they did. I just liked them. They're great friends, but everyone posted about me by proximity. Then the Coachella incident happened. All of a sudden, people gave me clothes and bags to carry. I saw the world on someone else's dime as long as I posted about it. It was not a bad first job after college. There's lots of money to be made in appearances. It was so dumb, but my dad, a winemaker, taught me you make wine or hay when the sun shines. You live and die by the harvest and never know what it may bring. Grab all you can while there's something to grab. You also put it all away for a rainy day. After three years of being a brand and three years working my ass off in Dior's merchandising department, I have enough money to do the thing I really want to do.

Every product I brandished was for my end goal. To carve out the career I want. My father and his friends have all worked their asses off for their dreams. I paid attention. I learned you plan, put your head down, and go after what you want. Wine's not my thing despite it being in my blood. It's always been music. Not performing but creating and shaping it.

"You can't tell anyone what I'm doing. I need a fresh start outside this media-created spotlight, and away from being a part of the '5'."

Five vineyard families are bonded through our parents, and we're all freaky close. We were basically raised together. My Dad and his best friend, Will Whittier, are like the Godfathers of these five families.

My older brother, Bax, and his four best friends own a winery called Prohibition. Very few of us can escape the pull of the families. And just when you think you're out, they pull you back in. There's a reason I chose Dior in Paris and not Carolina Herrera in New York. More distance from the pull. I love them, but they're a bit overwhelming.

I smooth my hair back in the hall mirror and approach the hostess and ask in French, "Déjeuner Dior?"

She responds in English, which always irks me. Even though I'm fluent, they always know I'm an American.

"You're the first." She leads me to the room. I stand there for a moment. "Merci." She winks at me.

"Dad, did you tell people about my plan?"

"Just your sister and well, I'm sorry, he asked about you, so I told Sam."

"DAD! Sam is the worst secret keeper. Everyone knows now." Sam's one of my brother's crew and like a cousin to me. I'm the youngest of all the siblings, and they're all over-protective.

He laughs. "Goldie is very excited you're coming home, Little Bell. She's planning a party."

She was my mom's best friend and remains the proudest of my aunties. I look at the ceiling, trying not to be upset that they want to make such a fuss.

"You know they love you."

"Too much. And don't you think it's about time I'm something other than Little Bell?"

"My darling girl, you'll always be Little Bell. But it's ok to be someone else too."

"I love you, Dad. Stop telling people things."

"You know there are no secrets between the '5.'"

"That's like thirty people." I switch the phone to my other ear and circle the table noting the place settings.

"Is it? I hadn't noticed. Ok, feisty. Relax."

"Talk later, Dad." I hang up.

I sit on a velvet bench and try to get my shit together. I came to Paris to find out who I was out of the shadow of my insanely sizeable extended family and my charming over-protective father. My mom died before I could figure out if I hated or loved her. I look like her, so everyone calls me Little Bell for Bellamy. The mother, who by all accounts was spectacular. Only her best friend ever tells me about her flaws. Hearing her faults makes her human to me. Goldie tells me she used to get angry at the littlest things and let the larger ones slide. That means she wasn't perfect, and I don't have to be a miniature version of her.

My sister, Tommi, always talks about how she glided into a room. That shit can't be real. And my brother, Bax, who was ten when I was born and thirteen when she died, tells me how wise and funny she was. And my dad never talks about her at all. So she either never existed, or she was a Disney princess.

My work frenemy sneaks into the room. She doesn't see me as she checks the place cards. I already moved some. She's constantly trying to take credit for my work. Looks like she snagged a sample dress from the newest collection. I'm wearing vintage, and that's the difference between us. She sees me and pretends she didn't move her place card closer to our boss. I exit the room, and she follows me into the hallway.

"Chérie, tu es divine." We air-kiss.

"Tu es si magnifique dans cette vieille chose. Vous devez être nerveux." Bitch. I look magnificent in this old thing. Vintage does not mean old.

I answer her in English, which I know she hates. "So nervous. I'm going to pop over in here and practice." I squeeze the mean girl's arm and turn towards a random door as if I know exactly where I'm going. I want away from her— from everyone for a second.

It's dark and smells like industrial cleaners. I find the lights and realize I'm in a large cleaning supply/storage room. This will do. It's bigger than a closet but not massive. I won't be in here long. I'm not a fan of enclosed spaces. My brother locked me in my dad's wine room when I was nine. Never really recovered. I set my bag down and pull up my speech on my phone. I pace, practice, and try to use my phone instead of my elaborate notecards. Ok, the room isn't tiny at all. There's quite a bit of space to roam around. My mind wanders.

After a quick visit home, I go to the Chicago doorstep of a woman who has never treated me like a kid or cared who my family was. In high school, I interned at Meg's film festival. I wasn't the little sister or the sad girl who lost her mom too early. Instead, I got to be Ingrid. Her rockstar husband is letting me learn to produce music at his studio. I want to help shape and form something beautiful for the world.

I came to Paris to get out of LA and California in general. To distance me from what I was becoming and be an independent woman. Didn't quite work. No one lets me forget my three years on the influencer circuit. Time to get lost and pivot completely toward what I want instead of someone else's idea of what I should be.

Being the youngest member of my collective "family' takes a toll. They've all achieved miraculous things and then patted me on the head. Music has always been my savior, and I want to give that to someone else.

I scroll through my notes and pace quietly as I say the speech. I loved the Dior perks. My shoes are exquisite. But the job wasn't for me. I do another lap through the shelves.

My back is to the door when I'm startled. I feel all of my curated positive air sucked out of the room as someone invades my solace. Please don't be a janitor. I peek around the large shelves and instantly recognize the man with dark shaggy hair. He slams his palm on the door and then shoves something in his pocket.

I'm not alarmed but oddly curious why someone as famous as musician Ian Reilly would be in the supply room in a French restaurant in Paris.

I've done a lot of research for my new job, and his name came up a time or two. Given my mentor, how could it not? If I'm going to produce and mix music, even something as poppy as his, I wanted to know it all. I made myself a student of every genre and era of music.

Ian does have one perfect album. It's deep, rough, and riddled with loss. It's more profound and lyrical than his others, and I know exactly where it came from. And oddly, it's his most successful. Nothing has compared to the album "First Heartbreak" since then.

He's moving from side to side, staring at the door. It's as if he's commanding the space around him with the sway of his hips. There's a vibe, almost like an electric current, drawing me to him and into his aura. I feel a little lighter just watching him, despite his evident agitation. He's humming, and it's filling my nervous heart. I don't know the tune—it's calming me down, but it seems to be agitating him.

This is a beautiful man whose much sexier in person. His Irish complexion is creamy and perfect, with a glimpse of red in his cheeks. He's incredibly tall but not as gangly as I thought. His blue linen shirt hangs off his broad shoulders. He turns, and his expansive back tapers to a fabulous ass. Damn. Maybe his music is better than I thought. His figure cuts elegantly through the space like a dancer.

He's running his hand through his thick, famous, russet hair. He glances at his phone, then puts it to the side. I'm watching like a voyeur but not a fan, fascinated as I stare at a man who seems to be entirely at home in his body and mind. Then he picks up a glass from a serving tray and hurls it against the opposite wall screaming, "Bitch!" As it smashes, I shriek.

Chapter 2
Ian

Oh fuck. I didn't know anyone was in here. "Are you hurt? I'm so sorry."

I turn towards the stacks of industrial metal shelves. There's a tall stunning brunette woman with a severe chic low bun. Shit. By the time I reach her, I'm already lost in her dark brown sparkling eyes and the slight upturn curl to her painted wet coral lips. She's fucking gorgeous.

"No. Just startled. Are you ok?"

Her voice has a slight trill to it. I don't know if that's fear or if she's naturally a musical sound, but I like it. She's a melody yet discovered, and fuck, is she hot. The tight beige dress accents her hourglass shape and was designed by someone who knew how to make my heart flip. And here, I thought it was dead. Turns out it was waiting to find a woman in a supply closet.

"I'm not ok, clearly. I just smashed a glass in a closet instead of eating my steak. So nope. I'm hungry and insane and now trapped with a stranger. You're not a serial killer, are you?"

She steps towards me. "Worse, I'm a super fan. I keep all your pictures on my phone, Mr. Reilly."

My face drops then she giggles. Christ, I don't want a fan anywhere near me. I'm so sick of being Ian. I keep fucking up my life in such spectacular ways, and I don't need it pointed out or want to talk to a fan about it.

She then says with a cheesy grin, "I have a tattoo of your face on my back. Will you sign it? Then I can tattoo your name across my ass." Then a bright, bold laugh bursts out of her. It's so pure it makes me want to keep trying to hear it again.

I laugh at her as she crosses her arms over her spectacular chest. She's funny. That body, that face, and that voice belong to someone funny. It's too much for me in my current state. Not fair to bestow that kind of perfection when I'm not ready for it.

"At least you have good taste," I say and extend my hand so she can step over the glass. I'm loving the feel of hers in mine. Damn. Then I grab a case of paper towels and gesture for her to sit. She's so damn regal sitting on the case of paper products she makes it look like a throne.

"Thank you." As I sweep the broken glass away, she looks curious. "Did you say trapped?" I pull the snapped-off door handle from my pocket.

"Oh. No. No. No. I have to get back out there." She pulls up her phone and shrieks. "No bars. Oh my god. What is this, a bomb shelter? Stone Age WiFi? Shit." She stands up, and her black patent leather pumps, with a strap and like a death-metal heel, clack as she scurries to the door. Then she click clacks all around the room to see if there's better phone reception. It's like she doing a dance holding the phone up to the light, then squatting low.

9

"Ian. Mr. Reilly. I mean, you, call someone." I stare at her and realize I know who she is as well.

I follow her on social media, and I assume she follows me. "For someone who posts as often as you do, that's odd, Ms. Schroeder, that you don't have a backup WiFi router in your purse."

Her face snaps to mine, and there's simmering anger that started long before I made a comment, but now I'm trapped in taking the blame.

"I don't do that anymore. And please don't assume you know who I am because of some stupid pictures, videos and posts." She sits back down.

"Same." I snap back at her.

"Fair enough. And it's Ingrid." She nods sharply and sits back down.

"Ian." I respond and put my hand out to her. Mostly so I can touch her again.

She grins and shakes my hand. Her delicate touch is more than I can take in my current situation. I grab my own case of paper towels and settle in across from her.

"I'm rather handy. Please give me that." She hops up and reaches for me.

She takes the broken handle, and I lean back against the shelves and watch her futile attempt. Good view of her ass, though.

"All we have to do is turn this pin, and it will unlock."

"You go, safecracker." She turns to me and rolls her eyes. Then flips me off. I like feisty. She grabs a fork and starts to scrape metal on metal. As much as I would like to get out of here, a larger part wants to get to know her. I hear a loud metal snap and "Oh, fuck."

I run to her. The fork is bent in half and stuck inside the small handle hole. She rubs her finger, and I inspect it.

She peers up at me through her long eyelashes, and I swear I can hear her heart speed up. I rub the angriest-looking part. "You ok there, MacGyver?"

Her voice is breathy and sweet. "I guess." She pulls her shoulders back, cracking us out of our moment. She abruptly turns away and pounds on the door.

"Help! There are people in here. PEOPLE! We're trapped! It's your fault restaurant. Get me out of here. Help! I'm in here and a famous singer/songwriter pop star is in here!!"

I laugh and yell, "And a very attractive woman who no longer fancies herself an influencer, but you would totally know who she is!" I keep banging.

"Not funny." She looks up at me and sneers.

"Little funny."

"AHHH! NO!" She goes back to screaming at the door instead of me. "Help! Anybody!" She turns to me. "Help! I'm trapped with an ego!" I stand over her, caging her to the door, and I don't hate being this close to her. We both beat on the door, screaming for a couple of minutes. Nothing. I grin. Things could be worse for me.

She clicks and clacks in a tight circle in front of me. Then she begins to expand the circle muttering to herself. It's freaking adorable.

"Why are you in here?" I ask.

"I have a little speech thing and needed practice. And to escape a bitch I work with." Her head swivels around, frantically looking for something. "Oh. Jesus. I'm having a hard time breathing. There are no windows. My breathing is getting thready. Is there enough oxygen in here?" She bends in half. It's adorable the way she's working herself up.

"You're fine. Breathe in and out slowly." I rub her back. She snaps up. "You touched me."

"My apologies."

"No, it was familiar and nice."

Familiar. I agree. Even though the thought is wild. She flops back on her paper towel chair. I grab a couple more cases and fashion an actual throne for her. She scoots back towards the wall of cardboard, and only her feet dangle over the edge. She looks like a little girl in a giant chair. She's spectacular.

I roll my hands in the air towards me. "Let me hear it."

"Shouldn't we be trying to get out of here?" She's clutching her phone but seems to be breathing ok.

"We'll have to wait until someone needs more dishrags." She smiles, and even that's too much for me. I'm about to be humiliated and disgraced on the other side of the broken door. She'll run from me once she gets service and sees my viral shitstorm. But for right now, she has no idea my ex-wife just published a tell-all chronicling how she cheated me out of money and the staggering volume of dicks she cheated on me with. I'm a joke outside of these walls, but in here, she doesn't know yet. I have one last chance to get to know someone before they know what an idiot I am.

"Come on. You worked hard on it. Someone should hear it."

"Someone?" She raises an eyebrow.

"I'm someone." I raise my hand. "Unless you'd like to conserve the air."

She smirks at me and then sits up a little straighter. Ingrid pulls her legs onto her makeshift chair and bends them to the side. There's some blockade of cool that just slid into place. I'll break it down.

I know about hiding behind the persona and blaming behavior on circumstances. I tried to be different with

Abbey. Hell, I married her to prove it was destiny, not a lack of moral character, ego, and youth when I cheated on Meg. But in the three years I've been with Abbey, I did nothing, despite all I could have done. I didn't even flirt with other women as if that would right the wrong I did to Meg.

I know the cheating isn't why we broke up, but it didn't help. I never want to be that shit heel again. My exie-bestie, Meg, has forgiven me and is incredibly happy in her marriage. And I got karma'd.

The Abbey book scandal broke, so I came to Paris to get lost. Hoping the hashtags wouldn't follow me. But they don't know international boundaries. #ianreillygetsplayed #playergetsplayed #tellall #ianreillycheatingmess #ianreillyheartbreak #cheatingscandal #eggplantcomparison #ianreillywellhung.

They all run through my head. Someone stacked them on TikTok, and now all the socials are cutting and pasting passages. Now, that last one, I don't mind so much. But my ex-wife ranked my dick against my roadies and crew. I'm glad I'm bigger, but she shouldn't have a working knowledge of my band's cocks.

I turn my attention back to the most important thing in this room. Ingrid purses her lips and traces a tiny imaginary circle on top of the cardboard.

"Seriously, let me hear it, please."

"My speech? We're trapped in a room. And I'm supposed to be having bubbles and foie gras. They're going to think I blew them off. I'll be considered rude."

"Yup."

She stands and gets in my face. "Yup?"

"Yup. All that's true. But who cares what their reaction is? They're not here. I am. Give me the speech." I gesture for her to get on with it. She blows out a forceful exhale.

"Do you speak French?"

"Sure."

She stands in front of me. I spark up my phone's translator app that I downloaded so it could work without WiFi. I push my sleeves up, and she stares for a second. Even though there are billions of pictures everywhere, there's always a look the first time I expose the ink. And it's always a telling glance, and her face says she's intrigued.

"Je pense que tu es plein de merde et que tu ne parles pas français mais que tu essaies de me faire sentir mieux. Alors merci."

She does a little bow. It's the sexiest thing I've ever seen. This woman speaks French, which is also sexy as fuck. I nod as if I approve of what she's said. Then I reach for my phone, but she grabs it first. She's laughing as she sees what I've done. She holds it up.

"Read it to me then, smarty French pants," I say.

She does. "I think you're full of shit and don't speak French, but you're trying to make me feel better. Which is oddly sweet from a stranger who trapped me in a supply closet. So, thank you."

Now I'm laughing. She seems lightened by it all, not as severe and worried as when I came in.

I stand and pull my phone from her. We're close enough that I can now get a complete whiff of the insane lilac and peony coming off this formidable flower. She's stronger than those scents. There's something to the steel versus velvet thing she's got going on. Like she could grow where planted. She could bloom under pressure.

Her breath catches when she looks into my eyes. Then she's off. She's racing in a circle, putting her phone in the air again, searching for bars.

"I seriously can't breathe. There's not enough oxygen in

here. Is there a window?" She flips from steel to vulnerable velvet. I dig her dichotomy.

"You're going to make yourself hyperventilate." I place my hand on her back.

"I need a bag. A bag, I tell you." She grabs her purse and begins to breathe into her purse.

"You're fine. We're not in a sealed chamber. It's a room with normal oxygen levels."

She peeks up from her purse. "You don't know. This could be our tomb. This is our tomb, Ian! At least I'm wearing Dior. I'm ok getting buried in Dior." She breathes heavily in and out, then buries her face back in her purse.

"Don't panic."

She stands straight up, and my hand flies off her back. "I haven't begun to panic. But needs are starting to come up, and I don't know what to do about them!" Her eyes are crazy, but she's breathing regularly.

"Needs?" I lift an eyebrow hoping to distract her. I spin around the room.

"Stop moving so much. You're using up all the oxygen. We have to conserve our energy for the long haul. It could be weeks before they discover our bodies." She's serious, and I bite the inside of my cheek, so I don't laugh at her.

New tactic-- I move in front of her and take her purse. She reluctantly lets go of it as I place it down on a stack of tablecloths. "I'll find you some air. The first thing they teach you in adventure school..."

"Adventure school? That's not a thing and if it is, it's a stupid name."

I put my palms up. "Look, I don't know what to tell you. That's what it's called. When trapped in a cave or a storage room, make a list of your assets first. What can we use in the cave for survival?"

Her eyes are perking up, and she seems more involved in my jackassery than her panic. That's a good thing.

She nods at me and hangs on to my every word.

"Over there. Grab a pen and some check receipts and write down what I tell you."

She does as she's told but gives me a look and pops a hip as if waiting to mock me. I like it, mainly because she's pulled her snoot out of the bag.

I say while shrugging, "You know if we end up somewhere truly dangerous someday, we're doomed. So far, your adventure skills suck."

She says, "You're a jackass."

"Hold up there, Wildflower." I'm over by the shelves and jerk my head back to hers.

"Is that a pet name?" She puts her hands on her hips.

"It is now. Beautiful, snappish, and out of control."

She stalks over. "Ok, pop star, I'll start a list."

I head into the metal shelving. "Oyster crackers! Score."

"You're way too excited about them."

"Bottles of water. That's lunch and dinner, baby!" I pump my fists and exclaim. I move around the shelving and find a door cracked open in the back of the room. "Holy shit. There's a tiny room back here."

"Shut up!" Her heels quickly clack upon the cement floor.

I open the door all the way and search for light. There are lockers and a slop sink. There's a mini-fridge and... "There's a bathroom!"

She pushes past me, and as she closes the door, she says, "Thank god. Don't listen!"

I step away and survey our provisions. Lu Petit Beurre biscuits. I crack one open, and they taste like butter cookies. I slide a sizeable unopened box of Comet cleanser to be a makeshift table between our two paper towel chairs. I drape stark white linen over the carton and arrange our lunch. Water, two packages of biscuits, and oyster crackers are all set up for us.

Her voice is light and bouncy. "I found crème de citron, some sort of tinned rillette, crisps, a pre-packaged jambon sandwich, and a bunch of what appears to be saucisson." She's holding up food, then sees the set table. She continues, "Those are baby teething crackers but will be perfect with the lemon curd!"

"Did you find some oxygen in there?"

"I simply stopped panicking." She bites her bottom lip, and my dick stirs just a little. Sexy and intelligent, a lethal combination for my cock. And the poor guy has been under-serviced lately due to the dumb as shit, harpy of an ex-wife. I turn my attention back to her, and all that anger ebbs out of me.

"Congratulations on passing adventure school." I place her items on our dining table and hug her. She's stiff at first but yields to me.

"Is there a badge or something?" She says as she sits.

"Yes, and later there will be arts and crafts."

"Can we make a WiFi tower?"

"Sure, just after we finish weaving potholders."

Chapter 3
Ingrid

We put the potted meat and the sandwich back in the fridge for a possible dinner. I bite the end of the salami and peel the outer coating off. When I'm done, I look at Ian; his eyes are wide. I realize I chomped into a long tubular thing, and now there's a heat in his eyes. I take a demure bite off the top and pass it to him.

He puts his hands behind his head and licks his lips. "Nah. Just gonna watch you eat that. It's all yours."

My face flushes, and I hop up to grab cutlery and plates for us. I cut a slice of salami, and he sighs. Then he says, "How about I watch you eat a banana sometime?"

"I prefer strawberries," I say, curbing the phallic talk. He makes me itchy in a forbidden kind of way. I've settled into being trapped in a room, but my body now realizes it's trapped in a room with him.

He smells like resin and sex. My last one-night stand was nine months ago. They used to be my favorite type of encounters, but for some reason, I invested that night. He said the right things, and I was taken in. After the inevitable silent phone, I swore off men. It was time to get the hell out of France and get on with life. Nine months ago, was when I formulated my French exit strategy. The one that brings me closer to my dream and further away from men. But Ian's messing with my head and my equilibrium.

We dine on our crackers, biscuits, and salami. "What would you have ordered?" I ask.

"Something with beef. And you?"

"Niçoise salad. I always have that, but I should probably switch it up."

He shifts, and his box sags a bit. He trades it for a different paper towel box.

"You're so damn beautiful."

My body freezes and burns simultaneously. "Thank you, but you don't have to say that."

"It's a date, and I wanted to compliment you. I don't ever do anything because I have to." He waggles his eyebrows.

What is actually happening here? Damn. "It's not a date." I pause for effect and then say. "It's adventure school."

"I had my first kiss at adventure school." He leans towards me.

"Counselor or camper?" I purse my lips and narrow my eyes.

He smirks at me, and his lips curl up like he'll swallow me whole. "Counselor. Now let's move onto the getting to know you part. Chocolate or caramel?"

Rapid-fire game. I'll play. "Chocolate. Beach or lake?"

"Beach. Coke or Pepsi?"

"Really? That's a question? Try again." I scoff.

"Fate or destiny?" He's quick.

I ask, "What's the difference?"

"Destiny, you can change, fate you can't," he says. Then he tents his fingers.

"Destiny," I say as I pop a biscuit in my mouth, covered in lemon curd. I savor the sweet-tart flavor of it all.

He asks, "You'd rather choose your path?"

"Hell, yes. You'd rather leave it up to a mythical force to decide your path?"

"Fate put a guitar in my hand. I certainly didn't put myself on the path I've been on in the last couple of years." A slow smile creeps up at the corners of his mouth and then fills his whole face. "Fate broke that handle, not me."

Oh damn, that's smooth.

I look down. "I'm scared of my next step, even though leaving Paris is the right decision. Doesn't make me more comfortable, but I'm choosing destiny."

"That's how you know you're making the right choices. They come with nerves and exhilaration."

"I've never told anyone I'm scared before. Did you drug me?" I tease him.

"Nah. We're trapped. Why not chat about stuff we'd never tell anyone else?" He shifts and crosses his long legs to the side of our 'table.'

"Tell me something vulnerable."

"You're stunning. I'm not worthy of this moment. But I'm going to inhale every fucking second of it."

I gasp. He's so blunt and beautiful. I'm having a hard time concentrating. I'm trapped with a scorching hot rock star. I need my purse again so I don't hyperventilate. His kind and alive eyes are fixed on me. I fold the napkin and then rearrange the salami pieces on the plate. And put the top on the curd. Then I look up at him. I'm back in control.

That's a lie. I kind of want him. The way he moves through space is effortless. Mine is calculated, so I don't make a misstep, but here's a man who's made many yet doesn't seem to lack confidence in any step he takes.

Chapter 4
Ian

We're going on hour seven in this room. I know all about her childhood nemesis, and she knows about where I buried treasure when I was seven. Every second I spend with her, she's lovelier and more attractive. "Are you nervous?" I'm captivated by her little fidgets. "I mean about the speech?"

"Oh, um, yes. The one I will now have to give in a board room tomorrow instead of over a jovial lunch? What do you think?"

"We should dance."

I need to touch her. I want to hold and protect her, and I've never felt this immediately possessive. She doesn't resist as I capture her delicate hands with my calloused ones. I know her from pictures and a little about her family in Northern California. But I never expected this, certainly not after the year I've had. She's a whisper of a future that doesn't involve pain. I need to know if she feels this too.

"But there's no music. If only there were someone around who might be able to make some." Her eyelashes are fluttering.

"Any requests?" I move a little closer to her. And the air is smacked with fucking voltage. It's like right before a summer storm—you feel it in the air, the ground, and on your fingertips. I gently align her hips with mine.

She whispers, "Stevie Wonder."

Ironic. After I shamelessly discounted the man years ago, I worked on myself musically and emotionally. I know every word, piano lick, and baseline. He's been my sound-track for the last couple of years. Fate.

I pile boxes on top of each other. I'm a tall guy, 6'3", and I need a tall congo drum. I begin a slow, steady salsa beat, and she begins to sway slightly.

I'm humming the beginning of Stevie Wonder's *Don't You Worry' Bout a Thing*. Her smile widens. Then she hums.

I keep the beat going. "You sing?"

"Not to anyone who will listen."

"I'll listen."

I grab a set of spoons and slap them in rhythm to my hand. She sways to the beat and hums a descant over my percussion. She picks up a closed can of Comet cleanser and does the shaker backbeat. It's sexy as hell that she knows the song that well. I sing the opening verse to my very best audience. And she joins me in the chorus. She loves this song. Damn, did I pick correctly.

I sing the line about how life's not working the way it should, and she finishes it with the next. The one about starting over in a new place.

I pull her closer. We let our 'instruments' go and keep singing. Our hips are in rhythm, and fuck, if my cock isn't getting into this mess. There's zero way she doesn't feel me. I don't care. She's going to ruin me. I can feel it. But it's going to be the path that fate put me on. I pull at the back of her tight bun, and nothing happens. I'm a little confused, and then she reaches up and pulls a long pin out of it. It cascades down onto her shoulders.

I need to step away from her, or I'll attack her right here. I dance back to my drum and pound on it in rhythm to the chorus, and she sings full out, and it's gorgeous.

Chapter 5
Ingrid

I'm all starts and stops right now. I curl my finger as he looks up from his drum and comes when called. I dance in front of him, swaying to the beat. He slides one of his palms onto my hip, and I put mine on his biceps. I pick at his loose-fitting blue linen shirt. His biceps are bigger and harder than I imagined. Damn, he's cut for someone so tall, verging on lanky. He keeps the fake maraca beat, and we fall into a salsa step. His voice is raspy but pure. He's raw and honest, and I'm charmed as he sings like this. When he's overproduced and poppy, it loses all that magic.

Even though his world is falling apart on the other side of that door, he's so confident. His ex-wife is actively trying to destroy him, yet he's so present with me.

He pulls me closer, then his lips are near my ear as he sings and slowly moves my hips in a swivel pattern. I match his movements, and he keeps singing low and sexy.

"Don't you worry 'bout a thing, Mama." He sings the title of the song. Shit, he's hot. I slide my hands up his arms and brace them around his neck. I let my thumbs trace a pattern on his back to the timing of the music. Then, as the lyrics swell, I swirl around in a circle, never missing a beat. Our feet are in perfect rhythm as he sings, and I let go. I pick out harmony and join him. He dips me and pulls me back up. We're nearing the song's end, and now he's let go of me. I'm freestyling and clapping along to us singing.

He wraps me in his arms with a flourish and spins me one last time. He lights me up—I can't explain it. I feel safe with him, right here in the confines of our adventure school.

"Ingrid."

"Yes."

He traces my cheek with his hand, and I close my eyes and relax into his touch. He's pushed some button deep inside me and freed me from all my bullshit.

"We should probably get going." He gestures his head towards the door.

I laugh, and his lips are on mine faster than I can process time. They're hard, fast, impetuous, and perfect. Fucking perfect. I don't think of judgment or pleasing anyone except myself. The room vibrates around us as I let my hands roam and his go to my ass. He gasps as he breaks away from me.

"Fuck. I'm not sure they have a name for what we just did. But it might be my new favorite hobby."

I flex my eyebrows at him. "Foreplay?" I'm desperate for him, and he doesn't hesitate to take me back in his arms. I wiggle my Dior dress down to my hips as my brain shuts off and the fun parts of me take over the controls.

"Christ, woman. You're in my head. I want all of you. You cool with that? I can't stop touching you now that I've started."

"You have all my yeses."

Chapter 6
Ian

I'm crazed to get her under me. I need to feel her from the inside. My tongue is sliding against hers, and it's real and raw. I grab the back of her head. I can't be close enough to this woman. I've enjoyed our banter, but there's this simmering thing neither of us can overlook anymore. She moans, and I'm freaking gone.

"Jesus, you're—"

"Amazing," she says with this little lilt, and it's driving me nuts.

I dive back into her, kissing her neck and muttering, "Wildflower, this is too powerful. What I feel and want to do to you." She throws her head back and gasps. I tear myself away from her, throw all our silverware and picnic remnants aside, and then push all the boxes together.

She giggles. "I thought we'd do it against the wall."

"No, I need to see you come undone. And that way I'd be too concentrated on not dropping you. Next time." I wink at her, and she sucks her breath through her teeth. I look over, and her hand is on her heart. I brace the boxes with a wall. When I'm done constructing our fuck pad, I realize my shirt buttons have come open lips. She's staring at my chest. Not sure if it's the ink or me.

She walks over and finishes the job. Her lips are on my chest, licking and lightly nipping. My body lights up with each pass her tongue takes over my chest.

She looks up at me. "I need you. And I'm seriously terrified at how much."

"Then we should dance." I attack her lips and unzip the rest of her dress while our tongues wildly chase each other. Her dress falls to the floor. She reaches for my zipper, and I see her lacy bra and nipples pulling hard against it.

Digging into my back pocket, I grab my only condom from my wallet. My crew gave it to me last year at the tour's end as a joke. They told me I was going to need it. I laughed and didn't quite get the joke, but they knew my future ex-wife was fucking around. I don't know if they meant I should use a condom with her or if I would be single soon. Fortunately, she stopped having sex with me when she fucked all of them.

Ingrid stops groping me and pulls my chin down to her face. "Where did you go?"

"Doesn't matter. This does. Can you read the expiration date?"

She takes it, and it's no longer a symbol of pain but rebirth and closure.

"We're good. We have a year and a half. I think we can get to it before then." I kiss her hard and long. My tongue swipes in and out of her mouth, possessing every inch of her lips. Sucking each moan down. I lift her and lay her down on our boxes. I grab a stack of tablecloths and stick it under her head.

"Aren't you the gentleman?"

I growl at her. "That fucking ends right here." I lie on

top of her, and the paper towels groan but hold. My goal is to flatten them. I let my hand drift to her thong and reach inside. "Hmm, someone seems rather wet for me." She moans and lifts her hips as I make contact with her clit. "Good thing because my dick is weeping and hard as that metal door we can't open."

"Let's do this until they find us." She hisses out, and I cover her mouth with mine while I explore.

"Good idea."

"Faster. Make me come faster and then get inside. I want to feel you."

"These are things I can work with."

I lean down and suck on her nipples through her bra and she bites her lip.

"I don't think I can wait."

"Then fuck me right now."

"You're like the most perfect date ever." I free my cock and her eyes fill with wonder. Ok, maybe not wonder, but she is staring while I stroke it.

She goes up on her elbows and licks her lips, "Is that my Adventure badge?"

"You're going to have to earn it." I stand there and let my hard cock flop forward and she grabs it.

"Ok, you passed, it's all yours."

"Good." Is all she says as she swallows it down. And I might blackout.

* * * *

SHE'S DRAPED IN A TABLECLOTH AND NESTLED INTO ME. I GULP THE moment down. We flattened the boxes, so we're sitting on the floor. I'm stroking her hair and kissing the top of her head. She periodically kisses my chest or arms. This is fucking perfect.

I say something that might shatter me, "Can I see you again?"

She doesn't hesitate to answer but also doesn't leave my arms. "I'm trying to become my own person and being on Ian Reilly's arm won't help. You have a lot of collateral damage of your own to fix right now,, you don't need me along for the ride."

I raise one eyebrow at her. "Explain, my beautiful Wildflower." Her voice is so beautiful. She has an innate musicality. I don't know if she knows that.

"The book. You can't be seen with a woman right now."

Holy shit, she knew this whole time about my messy life. I pull her closer, taking in her shiny, rich brown hair's fresh and intoxicating scent.

I smile and say, "What do you know about the book?"

"All of it. I turned down an advanced reader copy. Not a fan of take-downs, but I know the details." She turns to me, and I caress her cheek. I gently remove my arms from her, run to the bathroom, and grab my clothes. I need a moment without her. I can't believe she likes me knowing the ex-wife drama. Abbey didn't rob me of this. This was all mine, and I get to savor it over and over.

I yell from the back room, "We don't know when we'll get rescued, so as much as this pains me, I think you should get dressed."

"On it."

"WAIT!" I run out without my shirt buttoned, and she's standing in her bra and panties. I pull a breast out of the cup and let my tongue show her how much I'll miss her perfect tits. She holds my head, and I want to make her come again. I nip, and she squeals. Then I dry off her nipple and tuck it back into her bra.

I address her boobs, "You girls be good. If you behave, when I see you again we'll have more fun, ok?"

She laughs, and I zip her up, then she turns and buttons my shirt. It's all very domestic for a moment. I kiss her softly.

We sit, and I'm running my hand up and down her arm, and she's cuddled into me. She belongs in my arms in a way beyond comprehension by a mere mortal. This fucking goddess is both afraid of the world and controlling everything around her. She's so strong and soft.

Even Meg didn't feel like this, and I thought she was it. Until I realized I wasn't ready for someone of true substance. And it certainly wasn't Meg. This space in my life and heart seems to have been reserved for Ingrid.

* * * *

WE WAKE ABRUPTLY AS THE DOOR SWINGS OPEN WITH A CLANG. We've fallen asleep entwined. She grabs her heels. The cleaning crew is holding a crowbar and staring blankly at us. My favorite watch says it's close to three a.m. We've spent thirteen hours I here. I nod at our rescuers, who are all muttering in French.

Ingrid nods and says, "Merci, ça devenait terriblement étouffant ici. Et merci pour ton sandwich au citron caillé et au jamon. Ils étaient délicieux. Bonsoir." I guide her out of the closet by placing my hand on her back. I growl in her ear as we glide past a slack-jawed cleaning crew.

"I thanked them for the sandwich and told them it was

stuffy in there." We both laugh very hard as we push our way out to the street.

"Walk you home?" Our fingers interweave as we wander into the unseasonably warm spring night. She doesn't put her shoes back on and walks across every grass patch she can. We don't let go of each other's hands. After six blocks or so, she stops in front of a gorgeous home and nods. "This is me. Well, three rooms of it are me."

"I get it, but I don't like it. I haven't slept that well in years. How will I do that again without you?"

Ingrid presses her lips to mine. It's gentle and light. As much as she means this to be goodbye, it feels like a new day. "Take care of yourself. Good luck with the book thing." She's soft and quiet.

"Good luck with your new path and wherever it leads you." I'm still holding her. I desperately want to keep her, but she was only mine in anonymity.

"You'd be surprised where my first stop is." She smirks.

"Shock me." I move her hair behind her ear. "But first, I'm not sure if you've heard this enough. You're tremendous. Not just other orbits gorgeous, but strong and so fucking smart. And funny. You're more than you give yourself credit for."

"Same to you. You're more than the sum of your parts." She grabs my crotch, and I smile at her.

"Shock me another time then," I say because I want more. Because I don't think I could handle it if this is it. I want to leave something unfinished almost leaving a hat behind that I have to retrieve later.

"Ian—"

"Shh. I know. Let me have the fantasy." I pull her closer. It's been a transformative night in a closet. But now we're out, I get it. I'm a lot of baggage right now, and she's hell-bent on forging some new trail out of the spotlight.

I add, "Or we can go back and live in the closet."

Ingrid's laugh peals out of her, and she fills the night. I kiss her again. She squeezes me and quickly heads to her door, and we're done.

I wait, and I'm rewarded with her beautiful face framed by moonlight and the moment. She presses her palm to the window, and I return the gesture with my hand in the air.

I turn down the street, determined to finally get my shit together. I want this moment to be permanent. There's only one way I can figure out how to do that right now. After that, I'm guessing it's time to disappear and write a whole bunch of shit lyrics about the perfect night, and perfect girl, that might be mine someday.

Chapter 7
Ingrid

I've changed clothes several times. I left Chanel on the bed and opted for jeans and a simple flowered peasant blouse from Anthropologie. I'll feel better in something that's simply Ingrid.

I'm terrified to meet Morgan Sumner, the sound engineer, and the rest of the band. I don't want to walk in there and have them think they're doing Jake a favor. Jake is my friend Meg's rock star husband. He and his band, Grade Repeated, built a studio here in Chicago to stay home and record albums. They wanted to be with their families instead of traveling to record. It works for them. And today, I get to be a small part of the process.

I've studied for this. But no one knows yet. I spent every spare moment in college at USC's radio station, KXSC, pouring over the music and dissecting tracks with every music geek I could.

Then I danced at Coachella next to Justin Timberlake. The photo changed the course of my life. It was all circumstantial. I dressed for whimsy, which is my favorite. It was thrift shop couture, but people made a big deal of it, saying

I was a fashionista and stealing Justin. But Jessica was dancing with us the whole time. The solo angle of Justin and me alone went viral. They cut her out of the picture, and the world became a part of my everyday life since then. Jess, even DM'd me to apologize for the mess.

But I rode the snowball down that hill, taking advantage of all of it. I may bitch about the followers, but they're the price I pay for getting to experience all those wonderful things. I am freaking grateful.

I made appearances at clubs, parties, and shows. I was front row at global fashion weeks. But the entire time, I listened and catalogued. I studied and stood by DJs sucking up all the knowledge. I spent time with engineers, songwriters, producers or backstage with different bands. The pictures portrayed me as a party girl, but I was learning. I also grew up on a vineyard, so I have an insane tolerance. Everyone around me would imbibe too much, but I was able to stay sharp and observe. Over the years, I've taken all the teasing from my brother's crew for being the so-called "it girl."

But I was learning the way sound can bend and stretch. Or how it can fill the background or affect a mood. Understanding how music communicates and bonds became my religion. Figuring out what messages in a bottle songwriters slip into lyrics. I'm far from musical, but my analytical brain supports that kind of genius.

Just a touch of Tom Ford's deep coral lipstick, *Twist of Fate*, sent by a family friend who has a freaky gift of picking the perfect lipstick shade for people. It came in a care package for my first day in the studio. So much for keeping secrets from my clan at home.

I lift my boobs back into my bra and throw my shoulders back. I'm the queen of fake it until I make it. I can

35

assess any situation, see what it needs from me, and morph into that. But this time, I want to be just Ingrid, not what someone else thinks Ingrid is.

* * * *

It's hour four of the same song. I'm captivated as this green-haired pixie floats around the board and lays the vocals into the music. The entire band is recording today before they lay down solo tracks. It sounds like a silly song about a bar fight, but it's about heartbreak and giving up. Remarkably, this message is wrapped inside the ridiculous. And it's beautifully deceptive. But right now, the song is off.

They've tried different approaches, currently working with a ska feel. Morgan groans. She's petite and gruff. She's dressed in jeans and a ripped shirt as if she doesn't want anyone to know she's beautiful. She's five feet tall and scares the shit out of me.

She presses the studio button. "STOP. This is shit. Fuck. Let me try something."

They're frustrated. I'm fascinated. Jake scrubs his face with his hands. The buff and tattooed Rob Westerbrook, the other lead singer of Grade Repeated, is jumping up and down and groaning. They're the yin and yang of this band. Rob is pure raw energy, hijinks and power. Jake is thoughtful, calm, and sardonic. They're both wickedly funny and earnest about their music. They just have two different approaches. The other members walk away from their instruments. They let the frontmen moan and bitch, as if they've seen this before.

Jake says, "Fuck it. Beverage break."

I meekly say, "Morgan. Sorry. Morgan."

She doesn't turn around. Eventually, she pulls her head-phones off and turns to me. "Yes?"

"You heard me?"

"I hear everything." She climbs on her chair, squats down, and spins it around in a circle like a child. "What?"

"Penny's Noodles and beer will be here in a second."

"Maybe it will help this shit song we've wasted three fucking days on. We're going to have to scrap it." I crack the door to the studio, and Jake tries to greet me warmly.

"This is Ingrid. She fancies a career behind the music. Be nice. Sorry, it's a pile of steaming crap-fest today."

I meekly wave my hand at them. It's odd. The room smells like the rubber backing of the rugs and men. The rest is woodsy and a bit like the glue that holds instruments together. Almost pine resin. I love it. It's intoxicating. He smelled a little like this. The man I shouldn't still be thinking about. The one I did in a closet. That was more like my sister-in-law than me. She's wild and uninhibited. It works for Tabi, but it doesn't work for me.

I keep picking up my phone to text him, but I don't have his number. He's a phantom pain, but I think he's there somehow. The man is gone but our connection lingers. I've got to tell Meg. It's strange, but it's not like Meg, and I are related.

My mind wanders to him as it does too often. What's he doing? And the world, including me, wants to know where he is. He disappeared, but I guess I did too. One last searing kiss as he dropped me off at my house.

Jake's voice breaks me out of my Ian fog. I have my fingers on my lips as if I'm trying to feel him again.

"Ingrid, yo."

"Sorry. Lunch is in the conference room."

"We call it the hub since we got couches and shit in

there," Karl, the drummer, says with a silly voice. He's a squatty man with a rubber face and a killer sense of rhythm.

Rob slaps me on my back, then curls his arm around my shoulder. "Welcome meek one."

I turn to him. "I'm not meek."

Everyone files past us. Jake smiles as he passes. "Prove it." Rob puts his hands on my shoulders and pushes me to the hub.

They're done eating. I tried to clean up, but no one would let me. They kept saying I'm not an intern. I can't stop thinking about their song. I'm putting the leftovers into Tupperware, and they're bitching.

Rob is up and springing around the room on the balls of his feet. He's super fit and cut. Short dark hair peppered with a bit of grey. "Morgan, fix it," he whines.

She's blunt, "I'd trash it."

Jake says, "What if we push the bridge towards the end, write another verse and fill in the space with a better riff."

Thad, the bassist, says, "Lipstick on a pig."

I mutter as I snap a lid shut, "The guitars need to be crunchy and move to a 136 bpm." The song keeps running through my head like older songs my dad loves, not the ballad or ska they keep trying to force.

Rob's voice is booming behind me, "WHAT DID YOU JUST SAY?"

"Nothing, really." I whip around, and my face is red because I didn't realize I said it aloud.

Jake nods and sits forward on his chair. He rests his forearms on the table as if he's about to leap.

"Come, little rabbit, let's hear it." Morgan stands, and her smile curls like a cartoon character with a plan.

I catch my breath. I smooth my blouse to my body and

hold my stomach for support. "Ska doesn't work...." Everyone nods. "But when you were messing around before the last couple of takes, I heard it differently."

Jake stands. "Continue," he says in a pleading voice.

I say it quickly as if my dumb idea will sound better faster. "If you pull the rhythm up and pan to the drums, smooth out the bass and crunch up the guitars, you could pull off a '70s vibe."

Rob jumps up and down again but just stares at the ceiling. "Describe."

I get excited and nervous. They're listening to me. Maybe all that observing has paid off. I know this is what this particular song should sound like. Karl begins a slow drum beat on the table. Jake flails his hands as if he wants me to speak faster.

"Put it in the pocket of The Little River Band's '*Reminiscing*' or the Eagles, '*Take it Easy*.' Twist it a little modern like Amy Winehouse's '*Rehab*.' Something sunny and dusty with all sixteen tracks weaving into some old-school magic to highlight the song's irony. Give them nostalgia that isn't. Because that's what heartbreak is really, nostalgia." I slap my hand over my mouth. There's silence in the room. Rob is in my face and removes my hand from my mouth. He kisses my forehead.

"Don't ever stand in the background again." His eyes are earnest as he points to my chest.

Jake's beaming with pride. He yells above the drumbeat, "When will you assholes remember, despite her klutziness and apparent disorganization, my wife is a fucking genius who can always find the right place for people. Fuck, I'm buying Meg something shiny."

Thad says, "No, I am."

Karl says, "Let's get her a GameStop gift card." He's

such a dork. Then Morgan speaks, and I hold my breath. Her opinion carries serious weight.

"Back to the studio. Little Miss Idea just handed us a fuck ton of work." They all run out of the room, and Morgan looks at me. "Text Meg, you two won't be home for dinner." Then she winks at me and smiles.

My heart is so full. Everything feels right, and it hasn't felt this way since the storage room months ago.

Chapter 8
Ian

It's been almost four months living among the Swanton, Vermont, locals. And they don't give a shit about me. It's hot, and I wish this fucking cabin had air. I've managed to live through the chaos of the book dropping and the constant speculation of where I disappeared. Eventually, I got more press for my absence than for her stupid fucking book. Take that, bitch. Now the media speculates I've gone crazy. People keep reporting sightings of me like I'm a yeti.

I am really fucking sick of myself. I'm not sure what the next step is. I don't know where to go. I know I don't want to go home or to that building where most of my stuff lives. It sure as shit isn't home anymore. I want to record, but I don't know if I have anything to say. I released a random song before hiding, and it did ok. But it didn't do what I wanted it to. It didn't find its way to her.

I have all these thoughts and rhythms itching to come out and make sense of my head. I'm a bit adrift and paralyzed. That's why I'm still here. Inertia. A body at rest stays at rest, and a body in motion stays in motion unless knocked by a great force. There's nothing to knock me, so I stay.

They have a Dunkin', so it's all good. I walk and sing. I play and think. The other day I sat in the grass out front and listened to music. I simply listened like I used to do in my bedroom as a kid.

I've written many songs about water and rocks. None of them are good, but it fills my day. I do that and think of a supply closet 6000 miles away. It was only thirteen hours of my life, but I'm somehow different.

I pined for Meg once, but not like this. I don't want to be anywhere but beside Ingrid. I want to learn everything she's ever thought about and then weave it into my own narrative. And I want to be there for the live version of every thought she will think.

I'm on the back deck, lying on a chaise overlooking the Missisquoi River. It's a pretty good river as far as rural rivers go. I've seen worse. Perhaps this is who I'll become, the grizzled bitter guy who never bounced back after his wife slaked her thirst with dozens of roadies and other musicians. I can never look my road manager in the eye again, and he's been with me since I was seventeen.

Ingrid seems to be the only true thing besides music. And I don't even know her outside the confines of our cleaning supply kingdom. She's disappeared too. I can't find her anywhere, and I don't have her number. No one does. I asked around.

I don't use my phone except for demos. I don't want to talk to anyone. My parents have the landline number in case they need me. Everyone else can fuck off. I don't know who to trust in my life. I don't know who knew about Abbey and when. And none of those bitches told me my last album sucked. I'm not delicate. Perhaps my ego might have been a tad inflated at one point, but that was old me, like a year ago me. Pre-Ingrid me. I'll bet she'd tell me my last album sucked.

There's a loud crash. I leap to my feet and land in an alert pose with my hands spread wide as if that's going to protect me. A bear? Then the distinct thumping of someone knocking. No one comes here. It's not easy to come here. That's the fucking point of here.

I'll ignore it, and whatever they need will take care of itself. The thumping continues, then a loud, jarring voice pierces my self-pity utopia. Of course, she's here.

"IAN! Ian Reilly! Open this door. Open the fucking door. I fell on your stupid-ass steps, and I'm bleeding."

I groan, make my way to the front door and swing it open—it's like she's been stranded in the woods for a month. Her hair is wild, with branches and leaves stuck in it. Her eyes are crazed, her face has actual smears of dirt on it, and sure enough, her shin is bleeding. And I didn't know how much I missed my friend. I pull her into a hug, and she wraps her arms around me. After a minute or two, she speaks, buried in my chest.

"Do you think I need stitches?"

I laugh and release her from my arms. "You did this on the front porch?"

"No. I did fall on the porch, but I didn't think the rental would make it up the drive. So, I hiked up your "driveway," full of treacherous rocks and evil little holes. And I'm not an outdoorsy girl, so I got spooked by some noise in the woods. I may or may not have tried to run." She pulls air quotes and my mouth curves into a broad smile.

"Sit." I dampen a cloth with warm water and soap and she pulls a stick out of her hair. "How and why the hell are you here, Meg?" My exie-bestie has blood dripping down her leg.

I pull off my ratty t-shirt and grab a clean shirt. She turns away but then turns back.

"I'm here to fucking kick you in the ass. And your mom told me... Um, that's a lot more ink than when you know, we, um...."

"Did it?" I tease her.

She smirks. "Yes."

It turns out Meg, and I are soul mates in a different way. She's Jake's everything, and all my complicated feelings about that are completely gone. As well as any flicker of a torch for who's turned out to be my closest friend. Thank God she forgave me for my karmic jackassery.

"You still talk to my mom?"

"If I have to, and this sitch has gone on long enough. So, I had to."

She stands, and before I can pull my shirt down, she traces the small watch face by my grandmother's lily, now joined by a tangled bunch of wildflowers. My breath catches because I never intended for her to see the watch. I don't want her to misinterpret.

"Is that me?" She whispers.

"No, Bae. The watch is all things about that time, not you." I evoke the name even though its meaning has shifted. I trust her before anyone else. "It's the idea of you. That there might be someone out there somewhere, who devastates me the way Jake devastates you."

She smiles and places her hand on my cheek. Her eyes fill a little. "Your real woman is out there. I'm sorry I wasn't her."

"Oh, God no. NO. Meggy, you were never that girl. I just thought you might be at one point. You never need to feel guilty. Not after what I did." She pinches my arm, nods sharply, and then limps back to the kitchen chair.

"You can never tell Jake I saw your chest again."

"Clearly." I grin. Even though it's splashed all over the internet.

"Who's the bunch of wildflowers?" Meg used to live in Sonoma and might know of Ingrid, and I want her all to myself. "No one. Sometimes a tattoo is just a tattoo."

"Fine. You'll tell me later. Grab your shit. You're done here." She stands and starts collecting my clothes. She grabs sheets of scribbled lyrics and stacks them on the table.

"Where are we going?" I cross my arms over my chest.

"My house." As she limps at high velocity, it looks like she's in the eye of a tornado, not an off metaphor for her. Turning and kicking up dust like a memory. I stand in awe of her, putting the pieces of my life back together as if it were her job. The force to knock me out of my state of rest. Inertia.

I didn't go to bed after I dropped Ingrid off. Immortalizing the moment in time when, possibly, my molecules changed seemed more critical.

"Look, Jake is being pretty cool with this crazy plan of mine. Start shoving things in a bag. Have you ever been with a kid who's cutting molars? It sucks ass. Wailing and drooling everywhere. Multiple outfit changes. And we're in the midst of it with Pearl."

I laugh very hard at the idea of this international rocker, Jake, trying to calm a baby. I stand and cross the room to look out at the river. She curls into my side. I throw an arm around her. It's intimate but very different, and the realization that I don't want to fuck Meg is crazy to me. I just want her to listen to me whine. She's right. She's not it, and

Abbey's not it. I'm not ready to tell her about Wildflower, mostly because I don't trust myself. What I feel can't be honest and can't be trusted.

"How long have you been up here?" She squeezes around my waist once more, then picks up the remains of my breakfast dishes out here on the back porch.

"Sixty-two iPhone demos worth of time. Mostly songs about trees and my inability to move towards hope. And—"

"Terrible heartbreak songs?"

"She's not getting any. I've decided to pretend she never happened."

"Well, I'm sure the songs inspired by our breakup were much better than anything you might have come up with."

I grin at Meg. "Multi-platinum, Grammy for song of the year and album of the year, and number one download of the year. So, yeah, yours was better. Now what?"

She puts her hands on her hips, and I see the mom Meg has morphed into. "Home. You go back to work and figure out things in our carriage house. Jake will hate every second of it, but he loves me and knows what he married."

"You collect lost men." She has a trail of men on her speed dial who confide in her. And she confides in them. I adore our relationship, but I know I'm not unique.

"I guess I do."

I kiss the top of her head. "Thank fucking god."

She says, "Rent for a couple of nights in the carriage house. I need a favor."

"Anything."

"Can you mentor a quick ChiKid thing for me? This batch of kids shot great footage, but they want to know how to score it. Can you play different genres of music behind a couple of clips, so they see the difference music can make?" ChiKid is the youth program she runs for the

City of Chicago, and it all started with her mentoring kids in the film.

"That's why you came all the way up here, isn't it?"

"Yes." She stands, and I pull her into an embrace.

"Liar." I squeeze my friend closer.

She kisses my cheek sweetly. "Ok. Maybe your pathetic ass needed a kick. I'm not flying to the middle of fucking nowhere again. If you'll excuse me, I have to hurry back to Chicago, so my husband can take a shower and jump onto Lollapalooza's stage tonight."

"Ok. Let's go."

She beams and raises her eyebrows. She always gets what she wants.

Chapter 9
Ian

I did her seminar yesterday, and playing for an appreciative audience felt good. They are nine-to-fourteen-year-olds, so it worked out well. There were four clips the kids put together, and I played different moods behind them. They saw how the piece changed with the music. I need to remember the power music has. I won't forget it again.

It's ass-crack early, and I was up all night playing. Just playing and fucking around with sound and words. This place has excellent acoustics. I'm on to something here. I'm open, and I don't want to mess with it.

My flight's today, but I don't want to go to LA. I want to write and figure out what the next phase of my life sounds like. I think I could do some serious fucking great stuff here. I even had a fantastic conversation with Jake. He told me if I needed to use the studio to call Morgan, his sound engineer and producer, for some time. That's a solid man. I want to be a solid man. Instead of a man-child struggling to figure it all the fuck out.

Whatever someone is cooking smells divine.

IAN: Hey, you up?

MEG: I'm married. Don't start. What?

IAN: What are you doing?

MEG: Pouring milk for the princess. She rejected six of eight sippy cups. Weaning sucks.

IAN: What made the cut?

MEG: Spiderman and Olaf. Nothing makes sense anymore. What do you need?

IAN: Can I stay?

MEG: In my backyard?

IAN: Yes. For like a week or two. There's something here I want to explore.

MEG: Sure. Oh shit. Olaf is down. Fucker has been rejected. I'll run it by Jake. Someone's staying upstairs. Don't be alarmed if you hear them.

IAN: Check.

MEG: Fuck me. She just "poured" herself more milk. Talk later. Headed to the office this morning.

IAN: Thank you, BAE.

The carriage house is set up for two occupants. Usually, friends or nomad musicians stay here. They house session musicians and visiting artists sometimes. The place itself is really cool and sits between Meg's greystone and the alley in her backyard.

It's an excellent setup. Everything has been painted white, so it's clean and bright. The ceilings have to be at least fifteen to twenty feet. The large doors where the coaches used to go through to be housed for the night are still there. They've been sealed, and the windows expanded, but the outline remains. The vibe is casual, rock-star comfort. The kitchen's small, but it's not like I cook. I stare at the tiny kitchen and scratch through my stubble. Maybe learning to cook will make me a man.

There's a sunroom and a little patio overlooking the backyard. It's got a stackable washer and dryer in a closet. But the best part of this place is the enormous dining table. It looks like reclaimed wood. And smells of history. It faces the big picture garden window. I grab a notebook and start scratching out something a neighbor in Vermont said that stuck in my head. 'Flowers don't continuously bloom, but they're still there, waiting.' She was bitching at me to dig up the tulips and split them or some shit. I ignored her, but her phrase stayed with me.

I'm writing away when I hear the other occupant come down the stairs. I have zero desire to be friendly. Gonna stay here until Jake takes the session musician to work with him, then sneak in the house and grab something to eat. I'm starving. A slip of paper slides under the door. I ignore it. Instead, I'm feverishly writing notes and tapping out beats.

When I look up from the song, which is really fucking good, it's been almost two hours. Shit, now I'm ravenous.

I grab the note.

Your music gave me the best night's sleep. You're very talented. I made these this morning. Thought you might like some. Thanks for the guitar.

I

Shit. Someone knows I'm here. Why the "I"? I fling open the door, and there's a covered tray. I take it to the kitchen and discover it's an icy but plentiful plate of pancakes. I toss them in the microwave. Upstairs has also provided juice, cut fruit, and white goop that's not butter. No syrup, though.

I bite into the most unique pancake flavor. I smell it. It's like a Christmas cake. The pancake is whole wheat. Holy shit. It's carrot cake. And the goop is like a cream cheese frosting. So, fucking good. I move the flapjacks to the table and scroll my phone while I devour them. I read my version of the morning paper, then dunk the last bits into the glaze.

I've read the Schroeder Vineyard blog, creatively titled 'Grapevine,' every day for four months. The man isn't on social media and probably has one of the last blogs in the world. I adore him. I relish any tiny piece of information about his daughter, like a reporter on a beat. Mr. Schroeder is my only connection to Ingrid. I know she went from Paris to home but then set out again. He includes snippets of memories about her, and I love it. Occasionally he'll mention a visit from her or something she said on the phone. But nothing today, just something about leaves.

My belly is warm and wonderful, and I flop down on the couch with my guitar, picking out the new song and writing down riffs that work.

* * * *

LAST NIGHT I RAIDED MEG'S KITCHEN AND TOOK HALF A CASE OF wine. I'll munch on her leftover Kung Pao for breakfast.

I make coffee and settle in at the magic table. I had another idea last night. One, unfortunately, about her again. Ingrid doesn't show up on Google news or her socials. There are a billion pictures and videos of her if you search, but the ones with her family look most like my Ingrid.

I sit down and pull up the blog. Today's was about these five wineries and the friends he's close to and how they all help each other with things big and small. He also gave me this gift, 'Ingrid always loved the lush vines.' That's all he said, and I'm going to fucking dine on it. He misses her too. I hear you, brother. My Ingrid fantasy is interrupted by another note. I don't run to it, but I walk over, hoping to catch a glimpse of this mystery pancake person.

I like the third version of whatever you're working on. It has more soul. Enjoy breakfast. I made too much, as always.

I

Holy fuck. There's a smidge of pink lipstick smeared on the corner. This is a woman and definitely, not Meg. She hates makeup. And this woman is listening intently. I pick up the tray and lift the lid. They're red velvet, and they have the fucking fabulous cream cheese dip again with a side of bacon and fruit. Jack-fucking-pot. Whatever is with this woman, she knows her way around breakfast. I finish them while trying to remember the third version.

* * * *

Last night's song was yummy comfort food. Move the refrain up and double the chorus, in my humble opinion. I made sourdough pancakes. (Yes, I have a tiny bit of starter with me. I'm a geek like that.) Enjoy.
I

THIS WOMAN IS A FUCKING SAVANT, BOTH MUSICALLY AND WITH batter. I can't help but be obsessed with her. What does she look and sounds like? I might stake out the door tomorrow. I want to talk to her. She's dead on about the song. Perhaps she's European or Australian because she addresses the notes in reverse.

I tape a note for her to my door.

Thank you for the batter and suggestions. You're kind of spot-on with both. You keep strange hours, and I find the mystery of it all enticing. Why the pancakes?
Yours in syrup,
I

* * * *

Ever had a Japanese pancake? Here you go.

Kelly Kay

Last night's song felt undone as if you were
waiting for something. What are you waiting for?
Pancakes are a thing I do with my father. I
make them to comfort me or when I miss him.
I

JESUS, THESE ARE STRANGE, LIKE MINI SOUFFLÉS. WHILE READING
Adrian Schroeder's latest winery post, I sit and think about
what I'm waiting for. His son and daughter-in-law are
launching a new wine using some of his grapes for their
own winery. I've had Prohibition wine before, it trended for
a while, and I was sucked in. Turns out it's really freaking
good.

Perhaps I'm waiting for news of a girl who's more fantasy
than reality these days. Or maybe I'm waiting to see who
I'm going to become.
I

* * * *

AND HER NOTE IN RESPONSE TO MY OPENING UP IS PERFECT.

Well, those could be lovely lyrics. Perhaps some
piano and light percussion to add to the melody
you kept trying to finish. I hope you hear about
your girl. I, too, am searching for a lost connection
that feels like something, but there's no time.

I

I FUSE HER WORDS AND MINE INTO THE CHORUS. MELDING THE two yearnings for something or someone more. This woman is twisting my brain. She's wise. She must be older. And she's made me an apple Dutch baby pancake. That's fucking commitment. I can't take this anymore.

Piano will be critical. I can hear it when I play. I hope you find your connection today. I'm striving for it again.

I

* * * *

Rushed. Here are my signature regulars. Floated on that countermelody last night. Why don't you ever sing when you play? Or are you a songwriter?

I

THAT'S IT. FOUR DAYS. FOUR SONGS. FOUR SETS OF PANCAKES. I need to meet this woman. I don't care what she looks or sounds like. I want her to sit and analyze what I'm writing. She's so damn insightful in these little snippets. The mystery is killing me.

I sing and write and play. But I haven't felt like it lately. I'm starting to want to lay down tracks of these songs. I hadn't believed in my music for a little bit, but suddenly, I have something to say. Thank you, pancake girl. Please knock in the morning. I'd like to have breakfast with you.

I

* * * *

THERE WERE NO PANCAKES THIS MORNING FOR THE SECOND DAY IN a row. Is she that skittish?

I'm sorry if I overstepped. I just wanted to thank you in person.

I

* * * *

NO PANCAKES. MY NOTES ARE STILL TAPED TO THE DOOR, UNREAD. There's no movement upstairs. I think I've lost another woman.

On the upshot, Ingrid visited her father over the weekend. Knowing where she was for even a brief moment sets my heart right. She poured wine in the tasting room. There was a wedding celebration for her winemaker sister with all the winery families. Sounds like Adrian and his kids had a good time. She's gone again, but I know where she was for the first time in almost five months.

Oddly, I'm now invested in this man's life. Ingrid is a bonus these days. I'm captivated by learning how he and his best friend, a guy named Will, spent the day trying to fix something called a gondola. I don't know what it does in winemaking, but they needed it and they couldn't stop laughing long enough to realize it just needed gas.

His life has a purpose. He's an adult. I'm a thirty- five-year-old struggling to be relevant, pining over a woman I'll never see again. And that seems to be my only plan. I need to be more like Jake, and Ingrid's father, Adrian.

Chapter 10
Ian

That's it. No note. No pancakes. Step one to getting a new life plan- asking Meg about pancake girl. I want her opinion on some riffs I'm playing because pancake girl knows what she's talking about. Meg has to tell me how to get in touch with this woman. It's early, but the chaos in that house rises at dawn.

She'll kick my ass because she'll think I'm trying to bed pancake girl instead of using her musically. We may be legit friends now, but she's always had a thing for the long hair. I keep it shaggy and head over to her kitchen.

"Hey," I say as I enter.

"HOLD UP!" She twirls around, wholly stunned to see me. She knocks over a stack of folded cloth napkins. "You startled me!"

"I live in your backyard. How startled can you be?"

I bend over and pick up the napkins, and she pours me a cup of coffee. She shakes some sugar in it. She pours herself some more and takes a sip. It dribbles from the bottom of the cup down her shirt.

She gestures at it, "None of this should be a surprise.

Where have you been? Are you writing? I hear things at night. You good?"

She jumps up and sits on the counter, a patented Meg move. Jake removed an upper cabinet in his kitchen to give her a perch where she wouldn't bang her head.

Canyon, her flatulent French Bulldog, trots over to my legs. I sit on the ground behind the island and take her into my lap. We used to be pals. She's licking and wiggling as if she remembers our time together.

"She still snore?"

Meg nods. "Do you?" She tosses a wadded-up paper towel at me, and it easily misses. Canyon runs towards it, sniffs, licks, and eats it. She's always hungry and not very bright. I take it from her mouth.

Meg says, "I'm not going to like this. I see you. Floppy hair doesn't work on married women who have no interest in your way-too-sincere pop star stare." She takes two fingers and points from her eyes to mine.

I sit at the nook in the corner by the back door. I stretch my legs out, and her stepsons run into the kitchen. Ben, the older one, is like thirteen. The other one is maybe nine.

"Sup, gentlemen." I salute them.

"Meg! You took in another stray? How charming." She throws one of the newly retrieved cloth napkins at Ben. The floor is becoming littered with her chosen shrapnel.

The younger one sits next to me. "Who are you, and why are you in our kitchen? Usually, the dudes stick to the carriage house. I mean, the girl can come inside because hubba-hubba."

I laugh at him while he elbows my arm. Maybe the kid knows more about pancake girl.

"I agree, little man, some girls are definitely hubba-hubba indeed. What's she like?"

"Meg, make it stop," Ben pleads.

Meg's voice cuts through my nonsense. "Ben, are you headed to Ethan's this weekend? You can fly out on Friday midday. You don't have camp, right?"

"Yes. I already booked my ticket, and Liam and Jillien have my times."

"I enjoy a system that takes care of my flaws. Are you guys here tonight, or is your mom picking you up?"

Jonah answers, "Dad said while he has to be away tonight, you'd need men to watch out for you."

I grin. He's safeguarding his woman from me. As if he needs to.

Meg rolls her eyes. "Fine. I'll see you later. Go, or you'll be late." They both hug her, and she kisses the tops of their heads even though Ben almost has her eye to eye. They exit, and she watches them go with a dreamy look.

I smirk until she turns back to me, narrowing her eyes. She leans forward on the kitchen island and rests on her elbows. I stand to come over to her. The backdoor opens, and we're interrupted. Meg smiles and nods to the person coming in, and I turn. The girl's eyes bug out of her head, and my heart drops to the floor. It's her.

The air crackles like just before a summer storm, same fucking feeling. Hell, my DNA crackles. It's her. It's fucking her. It's the woman, other than the pancake girl I dream of every goddamned night and beat off to every morning. The woman I scan the "news" for every day in the shape of her father's blog. Ingrid Schroeder is the only woman my dick and heart want to be with.

Her stunning face is pale, but the rest of her is perfect in tight dark-wash jeans that hug all the angles and curves of my chestnut-haired goddess. Her eyes are popping light fireworks on a distant horizon, and I'm drawn to her. Meg doesn't even notice the two of us suspended in the moment.

I'm a whisper from her face. "How?" I want to touch her and kiss her immediately. My hands twitch.

"Ian." Her voice is breathy and laced with tomorrows.

"Yes, Ingrid. How?" Her hand goes to my chest. I'm overwhelmed at how my entire being is in harmony, in an instant. Meg brings calm to my life, but Ingrid is all-encompassing peace. She smiles, and all of my senses wake up, but my dick, unfortunately, responds as well. He's so damn happy to see her.

"I don't know how or why, but I'm so happy to see you. To know you're ok." Her words are delicate and soft but sure of themselves.

My heart flips that she cares. She might have thought about me as much as I fucking obsessed over her. Worst mistake ever, not getting her number. Fucking ex-wife took away my swagger for a moment. But she's here in front of me.

Meg interrupts us by standing on the other side of Ingrid's arm with her face between us. She sips her coffee.

"What's happening here? Ingrid. What do you need?" She shakes her head and steps back from me. Ingrid's hand slowly leaves my body until our soul point of contact are our eyes. And our sole point of contact is her fingertip. Finally, she turns towards Meg, breaking the spell.

She stutters as if embarrassed, "I need pancake eggs...." My eyebrows shoot up into my hairline. And my fucking world flips again.

"YOU'RE pancake girl!? You were signing your notes, not addressing them to me. I." I facepalm, then look directly at her.

"Oh. Shit. You're the music." She shakes her head. The

two women who rule the thoughts of my day are the same woman. "I didn't know."

"I assumed, or you'd possibly have said hello." I grin at her, and Meg smacks my arm. I turn to her. "What?"

She hands Ingrid some eggs and says, "There you go. Jake said they're starting in an hour. You can see how the master is woven together."

My head spins to her. "You're mixing?"

That's her path? My path. Music.

"Learning. Producing hopefully." And another piece snaps into place. She knew exactly what she was doing when she commented on my music.

Her lips curl at the corners, and she turns to leave. I want to run away and buy a giant Winnebago where all we do is fuck and eat pancakes. She can mix all my music if she agrees to the camper plan. She turns back, her cherry-red lips still in a hopelessly large smile.

"See you around, neighbor." And she leaves, and I stare at the door.

Meg hits me again. Her voice is sharp. "Do not fuck Ingrid."

I pretend to pledge her an impossible task, "I promise not to fuck Ingrid...." But I can't lie to Meg. I close my eyes tight as I say the next word, "...again."

"WHAT ARE YOU TALKING ABOUT, Ian Reilly?"

I put my hands up to try and calm her as she rounds the kitchen island and punches my arm.

"Not here. Five months ago! It was Paris. She was everything. I didn't know you knew her."

"She's my ward!" Meg screams.

I back away from her. "Ok, settle down there, Bridgerton. Your ward?"

"I'm watching out for her. I always have." And then it

dawns on her how odd this is. Her eyes slowly close as she puts her hand over her mouth. She talks from behind it.

"Ew. You slept with Ingrid and me."

I talk to her calmly as if I were a hostage negotiator or a flight attendant during turbulence.

"Meg, I didn't know your connection. She knew it was me, so maybe hammer her a little bit and stop smacking me. We got locked in a storage room in Paris for twelve hours. It just happened. It was the day the book dropped. You and I don't think of each other like that anymore."

She looks at me sideways as she heads back to the coffee pot. "You're right. You're like a dumbass brother to me."

"Exactly, nutjob."

"Watch it."

I grin. She holds her mug close to her chest, and there's a comfortable silence. I've missed just existing with other people. Despite our past, Meg gets my head to settle down faster than any dope I can get my hands on. She's just a different drug to me now.

She says, "Do you think of Ingrid that way?"

I blow my hair out of my face and admit something I thought was simply loneliness after my shitshow of a divorce.

"All the fucking time. I can't stop since the day we met. We were in that closet for thirteen hours. And sex was only for like an hour."

"How many?" I smirk, knowing precisely what she means. I flop back down on the kitchen chair.

"Fourteen or so."

"You already wrote more songs about her than me?!"

I say, "Yes, but I've only released one."

"Hold up! Glitter Girl?"

"Aww, you listened." I randomly released it, hoping she'd reach out. It was a desperate move after Paris.

"And you have a problem. Do not pursue this if you're going to be all Ian about it. No flaky. No cheating. No denying her feelings or your own. And you have to tell her about sleeping with me."

She's always been daffy and occasionally clueless. "The world knows we slept together. I have six Grammys to prove it."

She flicks her thumb against her teeth, then turns and pulls the coffee pot. Facing me, she pours a new mug of coffee, for I assume Jake. She doesn't look but leans back to place the coffee on the counter. It's happening, and I can't stop it. The cup is a couple of inches short of the counter behind her and crashes to the floor. Just as this happens, her husband walks into the kitchen.

"Ah, the sounds of Meg in the morning." I laugh and nod. He's a good man. "Don't move, my love. I'm guessing you're barefoot." She nods. He leans over and kisses her very romantically.

Then he turns to me. "Mine," he growls. I don't know if he truly hates me or if pretending I'm a rival is simply fun. I never really had a chance. They're fated.

"All yours." I put my hands up.

"He banged Ingrid." My eyes shoot to Meg. "What? You know I'm not good holding stuff from Jake." She shakes her head and puts her hands up like that's going to exonerate her.

"Cool, we have like a fucking Noel Coward play around here. A scintillating Gossip Girl episode. Perhaps we get my ex-wife to take up space in the attic?"

He reaches for the broom and hands it to me. Then he walks behind the island and lifts her up onto his shoulder.

She's losing it, and her colossal laugh fills this room and the next one. He glides past me.

He smacks her ass. "Mine." I grin and begin to sweep the broken ceramic, and he says, "And we have a toddler, so sweep it up real good there, Pretty boy Popstar douchebag."

I break out laughing at the name he used to call me by when he and Meg were just friends. Despite being in love with her, he was insanely pissed off at me and my behavior for a while.

I toss back him, "Gotcha Crotchety Old Rock Star."

"Rock God." He's laughing while he speaks.

As they leave the room, Meg lifts her head and yells, "Does she devastate you?"

Jake doesn't wait for an answer before they head into the living room. But for the first time in my life, the answer is yes.

Chapter 11
Ingrid

The stairs creak under every footfall. I'm panting as I enter the house and slam the door. As if that will stop him from being here. I've got a lot of excess adrenaline. I don't know what to do with it.

I've never been happier or more terrified of anything in my life. I made the man pancakes and critiqued his playing. I thought it was some journeyman session, dude. I thought he was older because the guitar sounded so seasoned. I didn't know it was him. Why the hell didn't Meg or Jake tell me? Oh god. Now I have to tell Meg about the super awkward thing we have in common.

I can't see him again. I can't want him. I have to wear a hood whenever I go downstairs. I'll sleep at the studio. My head is clouded. I'd finally shoved down all the thoughts and hopes of him that dominated both my REM and my awake cycles for months way down deep.

Now all of those thoughts are running amok in my head. He's not living rent-free but certainly subletting my brain. Jesus. How can he be here? How can I have cooked for him?

That smell. My un-drycleaned Dior dress lives in a large Ziplock in my suitcase to preserve his scent. I might have slept with it once or twice, then realized I was a freak. I mean, like borderline Dateline material. So, I put it back into its sealed bag and hid it in my suitcase. I had a handle on it until now.

The sunlight streams in the window, and I sit cross-legged below it. I'll hide. Seems logical. Eventually, he'll leave, right?

There's a banging at the door, and that voice teen girls dream of. "Open the door, Ingrid."

I clear my throat. "Cleaning service. She's not home."

He guffaws. I wasn't trying to be funny. He turns the knob. I didn't lock the door, and I'm hiding. That's like hiding 101. Lock the door of the place you're hiding. Dammit.

He steps through the door with the sun at his back, and I can't make out his face. But he clearly sees me sitting in the middle of the room, ducking just under the windows. He folds his arms across his chest.

Then the sun recedes, and I can't mistake the smirk on his face. It's mischief and mayhem in a perfectly symmetrical set of lips. I exhale. He found me.

"Awful jumpy, Wildflower." My shoulders make their way back to their normal position. I cross my legs and sit up completely.

He sits across from me on the floor. His smirk is my undoing.

We stare at each other, and I crack a wider smile as he licks his lips. Oh man, do I want those lips back on me. Everything I've guided my life on in the last sixteen months goes out the window as I stare at him. He moves slowly as if I'm a chipmunk that can be scared off. His hand reaches for me, and my breath catches. He tugs, and I look down at my hands.

"Hand me the carton of eggs, and no one gets hurt." I snicker at him. The eggs are placed to the side, and he pulls me to stand. I submit to my desire and him.

There's no doubt or hesitation as he takes me in his arms. His mouth is on mine, aggressive and hot. His kiss is urgent and desperate but not as desperate as mine. Our tongues crash into each other's mouths. That's not enough for me. I jump up and hitch my legs around his hips, and he groans. He's so hard already. I know how big that thing can get, and I want it now. I flex my hips, seeking friction and a closer connection.

"Christ, it's irrational how much I fucking missed you." He gasps against my lips.

"Me too. And..." He forces my head back, kissing and sucking on my neck, and my words fail me.

"Fucking now, talking later." He walks towards my little bedroom but misses the door, and I'm thrust up against the wall. We both groan as I frantically grind down on him. I'm aching for him as he thrusts into me, and I might come with our clothes on. He's raising me up and down on his cock and trying to find relief.

"Ingrid, I've never wanted anyone how I want you."

"Same. Now shut up and kiss me again."

His mouth is on mine with such force I'm shocked my head doesn't dent the wall. He doesn't stop, but he does finally finds the doorway. We make it to the bed and stop abruptly when his knees hit the bed frame. He tosses me on the bed, and his hair and eyes are wild. They're dark and hooded, and I want to capture every second of this in my memory. There's no rational thought, only lust. Everything is lost except those eyes and this ache in between my legs. He flips his shirt off and stares at me, licking his lips.

"Why aren't you naked? I want to see all of you, right fucking now." I grin and unbutton my shirt. I'm supposed to be headed to work in an hour. That's not happening today because I only want to lick this man for the next eight to ten hours.

I get up on my knees and toss my shirt to the side. He hisses at the sight of my orange bra. I love orange. I think he'll like what's on the bottom more. I stand on my bed, and he stares up while he steps out of his jeans and boxer briefs. He strokes himself, and I'm lost in the rhythm of watching him tug on his tremendous cock. I walk to the edge of the bed and wiggle my jeans off my hips.

"Fucking commando. Jesus, you're hot." I forgot to do laundry. He moves to me, then his hands are on my ass as he rakes me towards his mouth, which is at the perfect height. I grab the bedposts on either side of me. He kisses my inner thigh, then angles my ass, so I'm presenting myself to him. I look a bit like the sacrifice in King Kong. There was no worshipping of each other's bodies in the supply closet, just hard stranger fucking. Albeit on pallets of paper towels. Now, I feel like a goddess.

He moans as his tongue makes contact with my clit. "You're so wet for me, Wildflower. And fuck do you taste good. "

I gasp as he sucks me into his mouth and grazes my clit. One hand leaves my ass and makes its way to join his mouth.

He looks up at me. "You're seriously all the fucking gorgeous in the world." He chuffs, and I look down. "You're like an Amazonian queen waiting to be worshipped." I laugh too. He might as well be kneeling at my altar.

"So, what are you waiting for? Worship." I grin. I really need to come. He's driven me out of my mind.

"Yes, your highness." He dives between my legs and spreads them wide. He's licking and sucking the most intimate parts of me. The tempo of his tongue sends vibrations throughout my body. I grip the posts harder and begin to rock on his face. His talented hands are on my ass, and he pulls me even closer. He flicks and nips, and I am coiled so tight. He picks up his pace and swirls in the opposite direction, and then it's a steady, relentless beat on my clit. And then we hit the bridge, the climax of the song he's playing on my body. He spears me with his tongue, and I cry out as his fingers strum my clit. My knees buckle as I let go of the posts and fall literally and figuratively into the crescendo of this piece.

I can only scream, "Ian," as I do. He grabs my thighs and pulls me to him. I slide down his body, shuddering and tossing my head back. Our faces meet, and my eyes focus again as he kisses me softly.

We're standing naked, bodies pressed against each other. His erection digging into my stomach as he licks his lips. "You're the only thing that will ever taste better than your pancakes."

Chapter 12
Ian

I've never made a woman come so hard she lost all sense of balance, but I've never made a woman come while standing above me. She's blisteringly hot. I haven't paid nearly enough attention to her perfect tits, but there's no time now. I place her on the bed, and her smile slowly curls up, lighting up the room and every piece of me.

I'm standing at the end of the bed as she opens her legs to me. "I can't believe I get to have you."

I crawl up her body. I kiss the hell out of her. Our tongues and hands are insistent. I settle between her legs, and she pushes on my chest, pulling out of the kiss.

"Condoms."

"Shit. I've been celibate since you."

Her eyes widen. "Really?"

"I'm not sure what you don't understand about how fucking bad I want you. You've invaded all of me. Every other woman is dull. Boring. Unattractive. It's a sad world out there for me when the only thing I find beautiful or sexy is the one thing I couldn't fucking locate. So, yes, no one since you. Except an ember spark for pancake girl. Now you talk." I raise my eyebrow and point at her. Her chin lifts, then she grins and looks off to the side.

She bites her lip. "Me neither."

I kiss her again and moan into her mouth as I peel myself off her. She looks alarmed.

"Where are you going?"

"Walgreens with the most painful fucking blue balls and hard dick I can imagine. Gee, I hope there's paparazzi."

I jump into my jeans, ready to smash my atomically hard dick behind a zipper. I turn to her with my fly open and my cock still out and bouncing a little to make her giggle.

She crooks her finger. "Shot. And totally STI-free, I promise. No one since you and it was a long time before you."

I pump my arms in the air, and my dick bobs up and down again. She actually guffaws.

"FUCK YEAH, I knew you were my girl. I'm clean but pretty sure I'm packing sperm. So can't help out there." My jeans are gone, and I'm back on top of the perfect woman in seconds.

Her breath catches when we make contact. I kiss her again, but the lust has shifted. We savor each other. Her gentle lips meet mine in a sexy steady series of small kisses. I capture her lips and take over. I slide my tongue back where it belongs, and it's met with perfect resistance. I groan as she arches her back.

Her voice is raspy. "Ian."

"Ingrid?" I answer.

"Can we be past this part? I promise we can be gentle and sweet later."

"The fact that you promised me later means you get

whatever you want now." I notch my cock between her legs, and she reaches down between us and helps me slide in.

I back up to get more control over this situation. My head flies back as my eyes almost roll back into my head at how fucking sweet and perfect her pussy is.

"Christ, that's so good. You're so tight."

She moans, "It's been too long. Harder. I need you deeper, closer. Be closer to me."

I look at her face. I'm stunned she went from fantasy to what I want my future to look like in seconds. I pull back and slam into her, and she gasps and moans in the most beautiful way. My dick won't last, so I need to get her there faster than I'd like. I want to take my time and pull like six torturous orgasms out of her, but instead, I push back into her.

I pick up the pace. The slapping of our skin fills the room, and I need her closer. I can't be close enough to her. I'm mad for her. It's fucking insane. I sit down on the bed and pull her onto my lap. She eases down on my cock, and we both groan as she begins to move. My hands are on her face and her breasts. They're everywhere at once, but our eyes never leave each other. Then my fingers grip her hips, and I help her speed up by slamming her down on my shaft. She's fully seated, and I fuck up into her. I'm so deep and lost in this merciless pleasure. I want to come now and then do it again. Clear all the schedules and calendars. Cancel the tours and recording sessions because my cock and I are booked up for the next millennia or so.

"Fuck me. Fuck me, Ingrid."

"I'm coming. Ian. I'm coming. Oh god. It's so much."

"I've got you. Fall apart for me, Wildflower." My balls are tight to my body. I'm so ready to release into her. Shit. I reach down and put pressure on her clit, and clamps down on my cock in the very best way. I groan.

"Ian. Oh, God. Yes." She shatters around me, and I clutch her as she rides the waves of orgasm. Her head is back, her rich brown hair hanging behind her. She snaps it all forward and stares at me.

She exclaims, "This is what sex should be!" I'm still inside her, aching to come. "Now you."

She grinds down on my cock, and I lay her down. I lift her leg and piston in and out of the perfect place, slamming into her harder and harder. She's taking it all.

"FUCK." I'm coming in a way that's unique to her. It has to be the bareback and not the soul connection. I'm a fool for her already. I need to maintain some dignity. Shit. My balls tighten up, and when they hit that sweet spot just below where I'm entering her, I jerk and make a noise that no human or dolphin should utter. But there it is.

I flop down next to her as we attempt to catch our breath. All I can say is, "Good."

Her arm collapses onto my chest. "Good."

We stay entwined for another minute, then I extricate myself as she says, "Got what you need, and you out?"

I laugh. I run a washcloth under warm water and drape a hand towel over my forearm like a waiter. I bow to her at the edge of the bed. "Shall I clean the lady up?"

She cracks up and says, "That would be delightful, sir. Thank you." She spreads her legs and is so fucking gorgeous. I wipe her down, then pat her dry as I say made-up French words.

She sits up on her elbows. "Ce sera assez homme sexy chaud. Tenez-moi." I jerk my face to hers and kiss her.

"You know I can't resist when you speak French."

"Hold me. Tenez-moi."

I whisper the words back to her, skating over her lips with mine.

I toss the towels to the side and slide into bed. She places her head on my shoulder, and I lean toward her soft, stunning face. People accused her of using a filter in her posts, but I can attest she's that luminous in person. Her cheekbones' gentle and perfect blush contrasts with her dark eyes and hair. She's the basis for all filters. Life through the Ingrid lens is more beautiful than anything I can write or play.

I move my fingertips through her hair, and she smiles.

She says, "Where did you go?" Her hands are cozily curled into my chest.

"Middle of nowhere, and even there, I was lost. I should have followed you."

"Perhaps."

"I kind of stalked you," I confess to her.

"How? I paid people to post bullshit. I haven't been in my own accounts in like a year or so."

"I know that. But you underestimate how connected to you I felt." I roll her on top of me so we're face to face.

Her eyes brighten. "Right? It's a little freaky. I can't explain you."

"Don't try. I was desperate for any information about you.

"There isn't any." She shrugs.

I sit up, and she sits on my lap with her legs wrapped around me. I clear my throat.

"And I quote, 'My girl's favorite pinot blocks aren't flourishing. She sang to those vines as a little girl because they were her mother's favorites. Maybe I should force Little Bell to come back here and sing to them, and they'll fruit.'"

Kelly Kay

She gasps. "Are you kidding me? You read my dad's blog?"

"Every morning like it's the news. I'm a huge fan of Adrian Schroeder. And his best friend. Can't remember his name, but he's fucking funny. He did a guest spot last week."

"Will Whitter. He is funny. My middle name is his wife's. He's family to me."

"They all seem to be family to each other. I mean, there's what like seven wineries all connected. He randomly talks about them all. It's a cast of 1000s. I can't keep people straight, but I like it."

"Five. Well, six if you count Prohibition, which my brother, his wife, and their friends own. We all grew up together. I'm the baby by ten years, but they're as close as anyone's blood relations. I don't have a single memory in my entire life that doesn't involve one of them. Will and his wife, Sarah, are like second parents to me. Their son, Josh, is my brother's age and rather protective of the women in his life. I'd be careful."

"Is there a flow chart or a class I can take to keep them all straight?"

She rolls on her back and laughs. "I'll make you a family tree. I have to go."

"No." I hold her in place.

She giggles. "I can't take the day off. They're doing the final mix of my song."

I sit straight up and pull her to me. I'm blown away. "Your opinions on the songs about you were actually valid and professional. Hmm."

She rolls back on top of me, her hair a curtain shielding us from the world. "About me?"

I kiss her and hold her cheek. "They've all been for you since Paris."

Her eyes fill with emotion. "Too much. Back off, Mr. Temptation. That's way too fucking much to take in."

I push her off me, one of the hardest things I've ever done. "Go. Get out of here. Jesus, I'm sick to death of ya."

I roll over as she jumps to the ground. She scoops up her clothes, and I watch her pert perfect ass scoot into the bathroom. She emerges, and I quickly shut my eyes, pretending I'm asleep.

She laughs, then kisses me. "Have a good day."

"Have dinner with me. Have all the dinners with me." She looks to the side. "Too soon?"

"A touch. Let's work with tonight. Takeout, or are you cooking? Because I'm not blowing my cover over you just yet."

She's tying her hair into a knot at the back of her head. Even that's fucking sexy.

"Fair. I'll think of something." I pull the covers up and close my eyes to let her walk away.

"Good." I hear the front door slam behind her, and her delicate footsteps head down the old wooden staircase.

I've always fallen hard and fast. A sucker for the idea of a forever. Meg and Abbey were both the wrong fit. I only hope I'm not mistaken. This feels different, not the same road I've been on. As if this road has been repaved recently, and new streetlights were hung. It all seems straightforward and smooth. Hopefully, it's not fool's gold.

Chapter 13
Ingrid

I don't even notice where I am until I'm sitting on the bus. My phone is in my hand, and I feel it buzzing. The world is floaty and bright. Jake's wondering where I am.

I heard the lyrics last night about his girl's crooked smile, and I didn't recognize him. Ian Reilly thought about me as much as I thought about him. Whether it's sex or more, this morning was perfect.

I want to tell someone. My brother's assistant is the closest in my massive brood to my age. She used to hit clubs and have dinner with me when I visited Bax. Now she's part of the family, married to one of my older "brothers." She's good with secrets, unlike my dad.

> INGRID: He's at Meg's! He was the musician I was making pancakes for.

> NAT: I'm knee-deep in an argument with a very sassy little girl. She's flimflamming salty today. Hold, please.

My lips curl up, thinking of her redheaded stepdaughter. The second feistiest of the next-gen winery set.

NAT: Sadie's settled. She'll be out of sorts until David gives in to her demands. But for now, there's no cookie. And OMG. No one could find him, and he's been in Chicago?

INGRID: Was in the woods, now here. And most recently, he was under me. DO NOT TELL BAX.

NAT: Because telling your brother about your sex life if something we do. Duh. Was it everything?

INGRID: It was tectonic plate shifting. It was a tsunami, an earthquake, and all the lousy weather things that can describe really otherworldly sex.

INGRID: But I can't date him.

NAT: Oh yes, you can, girl. Look, my heart is totally David's, but that man is delicious.

INGRID: You'll be happy to know he is actually delicious.

NAT: Blush.

INGRID: My stomach is fizzy. My blood is buzzing and snapping under my skin. I'm a bowl of Rice Krispies of lust and emotion.

NAT: Ride the wave and him. But still do the engineering thing. Don't stop learning or striving for that because he's good in bed.

INGRID: I won't. I promise. But here's a secret. He's good out of bed too.

NAT: You're in trouble. Jesus. Sadie's climbing the kitchen counter now.

> INGRID: Love to David. Kiss the tiny Irish hellion for me.

* * * *

Morgan looks up. "Where the fuck you been?"

She doesn't scare me anymore. I say, "Fucking," Then clamp my hand over my mouth because I can't believe I said it.

There's a pause. I stare at her. Her green-black pixie cut looks fresh. I concentrate on her hair so I don't have to look at her piercing crystal eyes of judgment. She tosses one hand in a fist in the air and offers me the palm of her other.

I return her high five.

"Cool. Next time text so I can plan. Listen." She pushes the studio button, and the sound fills the room. It's haunting and so beautiful. These two men harmonize about the agony of knowing things could be different, but no one bothers to change it. The lyrics are tricky. It could be interpreted that someone's in love, but it's actually about giving up on love. I have an idea.

I offer up an idea. "I want Rob's voice on the chorus to be dreamier. Truly haunting, but leave Jake's where it is."

Morgan nods and grins, "Girl, you're fucking made for this. That's an awesome idea. Sometimes these men kill me." She interrupts them. "We're switching it up."

She puts a different mike on the shock mount and removes the foam. I'm holding up the door frame when she elegantly gestures to me.

Jake smirks. "Well. Well. Well. You know our houseguest?"

Rob nods. Oh god. They know. Rob's in my face. "No

precious little angel, baby engineering savant. You don't know anything but our music. You live here now. No more going back to the multiplatinum pretty boy. Do not make his music. Do ours. Only ours. Enjoy your life here chained to our studio while you finish our album." Everyone laughs as Rob pretends to tie me to the door. "There. That should hold. Now. Why the nakey mike. Wanna hear my mouth breathing?"

Morgan shrugs. "It's the savant's idea to make you sound spooky."

He coos at me, "Baby angel savant. Let's try it." I smile and look at the floor. Maybe it's a dumb idea. "Baby angel savant, lift that chin. Take credit for the good and the bad. Apologize when something doesn't work, but always try. Failing is part of this business."

Jake says, "Your wacked take on our sound is genius. It won't be for everyone, but we're lucky you stumbled into my carriage house."

They all clap, and I bow. Then return to the board and set the levels for the new mike.

"Hey, Rob, sing the first line of the chorus?" I clip it and throw the playback into the studio. They all cheer, and Rob does a split in the air. He's got four or five children and a tattooed rock god body. His wife has issues, apparently, but he's always so chipper you wouldn't know it.

Jake pushes his glasses back up his nose and signals. Morgan slips back out of the studio and into the booth with me. The take is perfect. Morgan lays it over the guitar and piano tracks and sends it back into the studio. They pace and listen, and when it finishes, Jake runs into the booth. He lifts me out of my seat and twirls me around. "Do you just hear it or see it?"

Morgan pipes up, "She's got problems technically, but Jesus, that ear is hep." I laugh.

Jake puts me down. "How does it feel?"

"What?"

"To get your first liner note producer credit?" Moran rolls her eyes, but I scream.

"REALLY?"

Jake nods and heads back into the studio. "Ok, idiots, what's next?"

I sit back in my chair. I'm not sure there's ever been a better day in the history of fucking days. My phone buzzes. He demanded my number.

> IAN: Am I supposed to lie here naked, waiting? You've been gone for days. Hurry home, Wildflower.

Nope. Never been a better day in my entire life. I have a nickname that isn't about my family or my dead mother. I have a man who doesn't care I'm actively throwing away an influencer's empire. And I spoke up. I did the thing I've always dreamed of doing. I'm pretty sure someone is going to get hit by a brick. But not right at this moment. I'm so making pancakes for dinner.

Chapter 14
Ingrid

The music curls around the back gate before I can see him. There's a blues slant to it all, and I can't help but listen. He's singing nonsense lyrics along with the melody.

"Buddy mayonnaise makes sense to the world, because all I want is you and some dijonaise."

I cover my hand to stop myself from laughing. I accidentally kick a garbage can. He stops playing.

"Rat or perfect woman? Either way, show yourself."

"I'm far from perfect." I peek around the corner, and he's sitting in the garden, paper scattered all around him.

"Thank fucking god you're back." He's in front of me, kissing me quickly. There's sunlight all around us, and I feel his heat and light.

He puts his forehead to mine. "That's too long. I thought you took off again."

I cock my head. "I'm not the only one who disappeared."

"True. But see, I knew where I was. I didn't know where you were." He holds my waist. "That's where you belong with me. It's not hard to figure out. You're a smart girl." He thumps my forehead.

"Wine?"

"No."

Panic fills me for a second. "No, you don't like wine? Might be a dealbreaker." His tongue tells me his intentions, and the hard length on my hip reinforces the point. I say on his lips, "Oh. You want to do that first?"

"First, next, now, later, last. I only want to stop if we have a muscle spasm or to replenish fluids. Tell me you don't have to work tomorrow and that you've stretched. We need to warm up a little for what I have planned."

It's seven at night, and I don't have to work tomorrow. They said it was a gestation day. See if everything gels. But that still won't be enough time with Ian. I raise my arms in the air and hold my wrists, stretching out. Then I untuck my Josie Natori lilac silk ribbed tank from my cigarette-cropped jeans and head for the steps. He follows me.

"I don't think I've discussed your ass enough."

I don't look at him but bite my lip. "Perhaps we can do that all day tomorrow."

He growls, then pushes me forward. "Faster. I need to fuck you faster."

He cages me at the front door, and I fumble with the key. He moves my low pony and kisses the back of my neck.

"Concentrate on opening the door, or I'm going to explode, and Meg's kids will see something beyond their years."

I laugh and finally get the door open. He closes it with his foot, his lips on mine. His touch skates up my skin, removing my shirt. I grin when we have to stop kissing to get it to pass over my head. I reach for him at that moment and whip off his shirt. I stoke his colorful mosaic skin. His broad shoulders and cut chest are almost too much to handle while trying to catch my breath.

I kiss an intricate Japanese design—words woven into waves with koi fish edging the tattoo out to his arm. It's stunning. As is he. "I'm lost in you."

He says, "I'm happy to find you." His fingers are tracing my jawline. I close my eyes and relish the feeling. "And now we're done with the worshiping portion of our evening." He lifts me up by my ass, and I wrap my legs around his waist and kiss his chest and neck.

He sets me down and raises his left eyebrow in the sexiest way. "You're wearing too many clothes." He pulls down his shorts, and his deliciously long dick bobs out. I stroke it, and he moans. His voice is gruff and low, his eyes dark and demanding. I've never been this turned on in my life. "Naked now."

I quickly remove my pants and lingerie. His kiss is rough and demanding.

He notches right at the beginning of me and then takes my breath away as he finds his way inside me to the end of me. We both gasp.

* * * *

"I'm ravenous."

His hands are diving between my legs as I stretch. "Is she up? I'd like to snack on her, then we'll find something to satisfy your cravings."

I flip over and look at him. We've been up and down all night. Three times I found myself entirely fulfilled by this man. It's about nine in the morning, and I really want an egg slider from Stray Hen. I lie on top of him.

"If I have sex with you right now...."

"I'm listening." He moves my hair behind me and smiles.

"Would you walk with me somewhere?" I trace his eyebrows, then his cheekbones.

"Is this a perilous walk?"

I laugh and straddle him. He's thickening under me, and having that kind of power feels divine. "Maybe. But I would think the reward is worth the risk." I grind down, and he groans.

"Ok, sign me up. You do remember I'm at expert at adventures, right? And you did earn your badge, so I think we're prepared for this walk." I lift up, grasp his full length, and slowly sink down on top of him. Divine.

* * * *

"MEET ME HERE IN THIRTY MINUTES." I PULL ON SOME SHORTS and a peach t-shirt. It's my favorite. It's all faded, but it says, "Never Go Against the Five Families." It's from a gathering the five winery families had after a whole thing we went through and almost lost our vineyards.

"We can't go together?" He pleads.

"No. I can't risk being spotted with you. No one knows where we are."

He sits up in bed, and the sheet falls just low enough to see the V and the beginning of the only thing that might pull me back to bed.

He strokes himself. "No. That doesn't work for me. You look too sexy in that. Do you have a kaftan or possibly a burlap dress of some sort?"

I laugh and pick up one of the pillows from the floor. I

threaten to throw it at him. "That seems extreme." I hit him right in the face.

"If I could make my legs work right now, I'd chase you. But it seems all the blood in my body has relocated to one particular area."

I kiss him goodbye, and he talks on my lips. "Ingrid. You have to help me redistribute the blood to the rest of my body."

I stand. "You're insatiable."

His hand finds the back of my head, and he pulls me back to his lips. "Only with you."

"Good answer. I'll see you in thirty. And bring your guitar."

Chapter 15
Ian

I find her in the booth of Jake's studio. We kiss, and her lips are new to me each time, like a never-ending puzzle of pleasure and fascination. I quickly grab a piece of paper and pencil and write that down. It's perfect.

"Best egg sandwich. It's so freaking good. I got you two. I figured you needed some protein." I flop in the chair next to her and see a white bag.

"Aww. You care about my sperm."

She turns to me. "I do. And in return, will you help me practice running the board?"

"Ah, the guitar." I lean back, unwrap the sandwich, and shove the food into my mouth.

"Yes. I thought we could demo that bluesy song you were playing the second night you were in town."

"You remember which night I played what? Do you catalog everything or just music?"

Working the board, she glances over and rolls her eyes. "Just music and sexual positions. Now, did you record anything?"

I slide my phone to her. She holds it up, and I smile for

face recognition. I don't want her to know my code is INGRID. Then she finds the files and downloads them. She plays them for us to hear. It's not bad. She stops the recording.

"Here. It needs this hook. Repeat this at the beginning and then before you hit the chorus."

I'm watching as she becomes even more vibrant. She talked about her family and fashion and Paris, but nothing has lit her up like this. It's intoxicating to be around. She makes me want to play.

"Does that make sense, or am I totally crazy?" She asks with a leading tone.

I lean over and pull her chair to mine, so we're face to face.

"You have some sort of instinct. Don't doubt whatever comes into your head. I won't. The second I start to see a flaw or second guess is when I get plunged into writer's block. I decided a while ago to never doubt. Forge ahead. If it's shit, it's shit. If no one likes it, then so be it. You can fix it all in post. But it's what was true in the moment."

She smiles and cocks her head to the side. I rub her arms. I can't stop freaking touching her. I want to record this song with her on my lap and my arms around her. I hold her waist while she's still working the board. Then I brace my arms on the edge of the cabinet, keeping her close.

"True in the moment. I like that." She shivers as I kiss the back of her neck.

"Good. Because it's just became a lyric."

"It's the title." She stands and turns in my arms. "Go." She kisses me quickly like an exclamation point.

I abandon the coffee and sandwich. I race with my guitar into the studio. I put on some headphones, and now

I'm connected to her in an entirely different way. Recording music takes trust. In the process, in the music, myself, and those who handle it. I trust her with this, which is different from wanting to sleep with her.

I tune my axe, then break into my first hit. I can see her laughing. Then she pushes the button to connect her voice with only my ears.

"Sounds like a winner. But a little young for who you are now."

I grin. "Let's see what you got, Schroeder." I prop up the lyrics I scribbled in the middle of the night. I was going to call it *The Best First Date*, but I like *True in the Moment*.

The red light flashes, and I play like she suggested. It doesn't feel right. "I'm going to start again." I do what I hear in my brain. It's hard to explain to people that it sometimes comes out like this. I've written a song in half an hour. And I've written some that take weeks. This feels like it's almost done in my brain, so I play it.

My mind goes only to the music. Nothing else matters when my fingers connect to the strings. I close my eyes and sing the lyrics I wrote and things that pop into my mind.

I open my eyes and see her standing when I'm done. She leans down and messes with the board. Then gives me the cutest thumbs-up. I come into the booth, and she starts the playback. I grab her hand as I sit next to her.

"It's good but could be better. It's terrific. But what if you tweaked the words?"

And that's how I wrote a song with this infectious creature. Four hours later, we have a demo, and she's mixed the track. I played some piano, which I hadn't done in years, then she laid some drums over it from a session musician, a discarded track from Grade Repeated. It's genius. I text the drummer. I've seen him around and ask if we can use the beat. He's all in.

She sits back and stretches. She hasn't stopped moving or leaning over the board. I was abuzz with her energy. I'm watching every little move she makes. She's collecting materials and rendering the track. She really is fucking good at this, and that's not lust clouding my judgment. I don't fuck around with my music. I thought we'd come here and mess around, then I'd trash the track, and she'd get some practice. But she's got this. I'm not worthy, but I'm going to try and be.

I see her beyond my infatuation, which scares me, but I'm ready. I didn't think I'd ever be again after the last two disastrous forays into romance. Perhaps I'm ready, or maybe we were meant to be together in the pocket of this groove.

She turns to me. "You ready? I'll meet you there. I can take a different route."

I pull her to me and kiss her. "What does it matter? Come on. Let's go together. Let's be together. I mean, we're basically anonymous. No one ever recognizes me. And you look like shit. Cut-offs and a t-shirt. That's not your brand. If you're not posing with billion-dollar sunglasses or on the arm of Christian Siriano, no one cares."

She lightly pats my chest with a huge smile. "I care. I'm not done learning and being out of the spotlight. And you, my sexy, insanely gorgeous, and funny man, are indeed a spotlight. Although, I don't see you like that. I never really have. Perhaps, I've simply been waiting for you all this time."

I slide my tongue into her mouth, and it's possessive and sexy. My hands pull her ponytail out to get into her hair. I need to be inside of her now.

I kiss her jawline while I wrap her hair around my fist. She sighs and gasps. Then says, "Here. I want you here." I quickly remove her shirt and kiss the top of her breasts before removing her bra.

I pull off my shirt, and her fingers drift to my bicep. She hasn't asked, but I know it's crossed her mind. I lay her on the couch, and she's still tracing the tangled grasses and bright flowers surrounding the watch and Grandma's lily. I answer her question.

"Yes. I got it in Paris, twenty-five minutes after leaving your side." She kisses me with tears in her eyes. "Wildflower."

I look down at her, and she reaches for my belt. I joke, "Let's not record this session." She laughs and pulls down my zipper.

Chapter 16
Ingrid

A slight chill signals my summer of sex is almost done. My eyes search the sea of diners. Bored faces of couples and business meetings fade to the back as I search for a face from home. There's a handsome man my eyes skim over until he begins waving. Then my jaw drops a little.

I get close and shake my head to get a clearer picture. Chiseled beard-free jaw, brown hair held back with swagger hair product, built and cut body where there was once was a squishy belly and a huggable "brother." But it's his dark eyes that are the same. The sweet face of Sam Langerford stares at me, smirking. He wasn't at my sister's wedding, so it's been a couple of years since I've seen him. He and I texted occasionally, but no one told me about his transition. I'm in his strong arms and exhaling a bit since he's such a piece of home.

He kisses my head and mutters, "Little Bell." I squeeze him harder, shocked his Winnie the Pooh-like status is gone. He was always the scruffy loveable man in our crowd.

He owns Prohibition Winery with my brother and sister-in-law.

I sip my water and stare. "It's still me, Little Bell."

I sit back. "Well, shit, Sam. Look at this. You're like a thirst trap."

"I know. I'm gorgeous now." He throws his hands up and laughs.

I grin. "You've always been gorgeous. You're just so different."

"Enough me. Tell me about this life here, and are you ever coming home?" He takes my hand and squeezes it.

"Did she do this to you?" The sentence thuds in the middle of the table. "Sorry. Never mind." His girlfriend ghosted him about the time I went to Paris.

"It's ok, LB. Sammy's still a little raw, but I decided to take care of myself instead of being a sad sack full of shit. She's gone. Not even Mel can find her."

This is shocking since Mel, my sister's wife, can hack anything and locate anyone.

He continues, "I'm in a tricky bit of a grieving stage. No one's heard from her. I fear for the worst, and I think that's how I have to handle this. Taking care of myself started with Josh forcing me to go running. Then basketball with David and tennis with Bax. Anything to fill my non-wine-making time. Then it evolved into CrossFit and Krav Maga."

"No shit."

He grins and says, "No shit. What the fuck are you doing here? Radio or some shit? Do you have a card I can pass on to the high school? Maybe you could spin the senior prom."

I throw a small piece of bread at him, and he bats it away, squealing a made-up Chinese word. "Cat-like reflexes. Baby, I'm the whole fucking package now."

I laugh loudly. He's the funniest of us, a shit secret keeper but funny. "You always were."

He squeezes my hand. "Ok, but are you taking on a new name like Daft Grid or BellMaus? Or spinning the greatest hits from the '60s, '70s and today."

"Not DJ, you ass.I'm helping produce Grade Repeated's new album." I look down at the plate in front of me and feel warm and fuzzy. He ordered me mac and cheese. It's my favorite, and he remembered. There's also some chicken thing I probably won't eat with vegetables. It looks too soupy.

His eyes almost bug out of his head. "Like a real job. You're all grown up, Little Bell. I don't care for it. That means I'm old. I'm going to end up that ancient bachelor in a velour tracksuit unzipped a bit too far. I might be a new me, but the forest on my chest will gray up and stick out of the front of that suit. I draw the line at waxing."

I wipe the tears of laughter from my eyes, but he won't stop.

"I'll be the one at the pool pinching waitresses and regaling them with tales of how I keep my skin so leathery." He lifts his biceps like he's showing off. I'm dying.

"Ok, I won't grow up anymore."

He shoves a big bite of salmon into his mouth and says, "You do that. My fate's in your hands." He chews, and I sip some wine he's brought along. It's a little funky but good. It's a Grenache/Cinsault blend from Prohibition called "Are You Happy Now?" I know it references my sister-in-law's favorite grape, and they weren't growing it for a long time. He catches my eye. "You, ok? Happy?"

"Very." I can't help but beam happiness all over the table.

"One of us should be."

My heart is breaking for him. His girlfriend was really cool, and they were perfect together. A raspy voice interrupts us.

"Interesting. You won't go to dinner with me, but this guy?" My head whips to Ian's face and his pursed lips. I'm not sure if he's jealous, pissed, or kidding.

Sam's up, and he's raw and angry. He's aggressive in a way I've never known, and he gets in Ian's face. I'm terrified of my overprotective new Krav Maga edition of Sam.

"Why don't you move along?"

Sam is huge when he stands. I mean fucking thick and ripped. Jesus. I try and stand, and Sam, without looking, guides me back to my seat with his hand on my shoulder.

"Sam. It's—" Ian's face is now screwed up too.

"I've got this, Ingrid," Sam says.

Ian steps back a bit. "You do, dude? You got this?" Oh shit.

"Ian. Don't."

Sam's head whips to mine. "You know this lanky muthafucker?" Is Sam on roids? He's never angry like this.

I nod, and Sam backs down for a second. "Talk, Little Bell." Sam doesn't move but stares at Ian.

Ian says, "You don't tell her what to do. What the fuck is your problem? And who the fuck...." Ian's face suddenly relaxes, then he steps behind me and addresses Sam. "You said, Little Bell. Hulking with an overprotective brother vibe. My guess is Josh."

I correct Ian, "Sam."

"Really? Not Josh?" I've told Ian all about the guys, and he always asks for a description of the people mentioned in my dad's blog.

I turn to Ian, and he grips my shoulders. "He's lost weight and is cut like an MMA fighter now."

Sam extends a hand. "Sam Langerford, and who are you? Why are you touching Little Bell?"

Ian shakes his hand. "Do you mind if I sit, so we can draw less attention?" Sam slightly nods. "I'm Little Bell's boyfriend."

My heart flips. I don't know what to do with this information. We've never said the words. There's no reason to define things in the privacy of our carriage house, but I guess it's true.

Sam sits back. "Interesting. You ready for the gauntlet for defiling my little sister? You fancy yourself her boyfriend. That's fucking hysterical. You're a funny guy."

I roll my eyes and put my hand on Sam's enormous forearm. "Sam, he is. And I'm happy."

"What do you do, boyfriend?"

Ian looks confused. He's been famous since he was seventeen years old. I shrug.

"Hey, man, I'm not trying to be an ass, but I'm Ian Reilly."

"Doesn't mean shit to me."

"I'm a musician."

"Bum, or have you done something?"

I google Ian and slide the phone to Sam.

"Datum, boy. Well, that's a few more hits than I get. I'm not good with names. I'm sure I've heard something." Sam has to be bluffing. He plays guitar in a bunch of local bands. He has to freaking know who he is.

Ian kisses my cheek. "This is the first time we've been out in public. She won't risk being recognized. And I got ruffled she was with another man."

Sam says, "Oh shit. That's why we're eating at like four in the afternoon, so no one recognizes, Bell."

I nod at him and Ian sips my wine. Sam toasts him.

Kelly Kay

Ian smiles and says, "My apologies for overreacting."

"Understandable. She's sitting here with an Adonis of a wine god and you with your measly kabillion google hits. I'd be intimidated too."

Ian cracks a smile. "You get it. I mean, seeing her in here with a male model of your stature, I couldn't help but drown in my own inadequacies."

Sam chuckles.

"What are you doing here?" I ask Ian.

"I heard the mac and cheese here was dreamy. I had to sign some papers at a lawyer's office down here, so I wandered in to pick up some mac for someone I know."

I shovel a massive bite of it into my mouth and grin. And he wipes my mouth with a napkin and settles back into the chair. He stands up and collects his to-go bags. I'm stoked for more mac later. He refrains from kissing me, and I appreciate it.

Sam stands and shakes his hand. "It was a pleasure. Now, never touch Little Bell again."

Ian replies, "To meet a piece of this woman's home is truly an honor. And even though I'm pretty sure you could crush me flat, I'm probably going to get lucky in like...." He looks at me, and I grin.

"Like an hour or so," I say.

"I speak for like thirty people when I say, don't hurt her. Don't fuck this up."

He clasps Sam's elbow and hand. "I don't intend to. Take care." He squeezes my shoulder and exits, carrying two huge bags of carryout.

I squirm in my seat and stare at Sam, pushing his salmon around the plate. He shakes his head.

"How long?"

"Six weeks officially, but, Sam, I'm pretty sure it's been

going on for longer than either of us can fathom. Only Nat knows." He pretends to button his lip with elaborate locks and zippers. Everyone in my family will probably know within the hour. He sighs and holds my hands.

"He's your Sammy. I see it. Let him take you out. You'll be fine. If he really does care for you don't let him hide you away." I wince. Sam still thinks of her as his soul mate.

"I think it's me who's doing the hiding but I get your point."

I squeeze his arm before he can take a bite. "I love you. Thanks for having my back."

"Love ya, LB." He winks.

* * * *

As I hustle around her kitchen, making grilled cheese for everyone, Meg asks, "Does he do that thing with his feet?"

"The rubbing back and forth as if he's trying to get closer to your feet?"

"Ok, women. That's quite enough compare and contrast. This is strange."

Meg turns to him and says, "Only for you. I was secretly in love with Jake at the time. I don't remember a lot." She winks at him. Ian groans and shifts Pearl. She's on his lap, and he looks domestic and perfect. Jake's boys run through the house.

"Grab your stuff. You're going to be late for school. And, Jonah, grab Pearl and take her up to her crib for me. I'll be up in a second."

"Why am I always the baby sherpa?" I adore Jonah's vocabulary. But I guess that comes when your dad is a songwriting genius.

The kids exit, and Meg looks at him. "Seriously, I'm not feeling a thing." She gestures to her whole body and almost knocks over a cup. She wanders out of the room, and I straddle Ian.

"Let's get some oxygen. I miss getting dressed up. Take my pretty clothes to dinner."

"You know the only purpose of a date is to get those pretty clothes off. Let's just do that."

I slap his arm. "No one knows we're in Chicago or even know each other. There was no fallout from Sam's meal. I don't want a Meg tattoo situation. I simply want to do something with you out of the house."

He kisses me slowly, and I nip his lip. "What's that about?"

"You do that to me. You make me want to do really naughty things."

"Stop fucking in my kitchen. Oh my god. Ian, as hard as it is for me to squash another man's game..."

"Is it? Is it really? Considering our history?" He shakes his head. "You know I like to bust your balls there, Jakey. All those years of calling me PBDB." I look to Ingrid, "Pretty Boy Douchebag." She nods and laughs.

"Just stop fucking in my kitchen. My kids could walk in. And shouldn't you people be moving out of my backyard?"

"Soon."

Chapter 17
Ian

We scoot down the alley behind Gentry, an old-school piano bar in the heart of Boystown. She's stunning in a yellow-flowered dress that flutters around her knees. She made sure I knew it was Nanette Lepore. You can take the influencer's phone away, but... you can't take the influencer out of the girl. I put on a pink linen shirt and shorts. And I ironed the shirt.

"Ready for our first date?" I ask.

She cocks her head and looks around. "You promise no one will know us."

"I never said that." She tries to pull away. "I said no one will take it public."

"You're delusional."

I open the back door, and it lets us behind a curtain. The room is filled with people and waitstaff scurrying around with cocktails and eggs bennie. The MC for brunch and my contact in this scheme is off to the side of us, and we can't quite see them.

We hear in a loud, gravely cheeky voice, "All right, bitches. Everybody here signed, right? Gals, no holdouts, or you're out! The waitstaff is collecting your agreements now. Yo! I'm talking up here. All eyes are on me, as they should be. Who didn't sign their life away to sing Sondheim and sip some damn bloodys?"

One hand goes up. We're still well hidden.

Ingrid is giddy. "I love karaoke. But do we need to sign?"

I shake my head 'no' at her, and my lips curl into a small smile as I wink at her.

"Ok, now we're all damn legal. No one leaves, and no one comes... or enters... until we're done. It's like death-match karaoke today."

There's a massive roar of laughter, and we giggle too. "Do not think that Gaga is here for a command perfor-mance. It's just two straight, cis white people who wanted to have a first date without a goddamn hassle. So shut it, bitches."

The crowd collectively says, "Aww."

"They signed NDAs?" Ingrid gasps.

"Yup," I whisper back.

The host says, "So if the urge to take pictures arises, remember to point your peepers and cameras at me, dahlings. I'm always ready for my close-up!"

I take Ingrid's hand and step out from behind the curtain. The host, Ms. Mac A Damia, rushes to us. "Aren't you more gorgeous than I thought?"

We air-kiss, then Ms. Damia squeezes Ingrid carefully, not getting their makeup on us. The crowd is murmuring.

I turn to the crowd. "Hi! Yes. Yes, and yes. We're dating, and you're the only people on earth who know that. You can take your NDA copies home and show people once we've gone public. Thanks so much for this. We can't wait to hear you all sing."

Someone shouts, "Honey, we don't give a shit."

There's a roar of laughter, and Ingrid lifts her head with a smile. "As long as you sing a show tune, you're welcome here."

We sit, and the men beside us swoon at my girl a bit. She is stunning and almost otherworldly. One of the men leans over. "Your pictures are trash. Sweetheart, you're flawless."

A platinum blond man leans toward her, and I can see her starting to relax. "I was YOU for Halloween!"

She laughs. "Then I should go as you this year."

He pulls out his phone, and she covers it and frowns. Dammit. No fucking selfies today. He looks at her and then realizes.

"Oh shit. No. I was just going to show you the picture."

She smiles and says, "Just send it to my DMs, and I'll see it there. I'm a bit camera shy these days." He nods and winks at her.

"OK! Enough oohing and ahhing. Get the vodka flowing, and up first is Gehart with...."

The room answers with a groan, "*The Impossible Dream.*"

He takes the stage as a waitress arrives. "Catalogue and menu." She tosses it down, and we order drinks and settle in for Broadway Brunch.

＊＊＊＊

THERE HAVE BEEN LOTS OF STRAINING VOICES, BUT SOME ARE really good. Ingrid is clapping and chatting with everyone around us.

I sang a stirring rendition of *Let the Sunshine In*, and was asked to take my clothes off. Respect. We've inhaled mimosas, bagels, and lox. Every time she takes a sip, I can't help but watch her lips. I squeeze her arm and make my way over to Ms. Mac A Damia.

"Thank you. For everything."

"No problemo. Such a unique request. I love young love."

I hand over my Amex. "Run it for everyone. Tip the staff well."

"You don't need to do this." They squeal in delight and shake their hips.

"But I can. And look how happy my girl is." They nod to the stage. "Yeah, but can she sing?"

"Hi. I'm Ingrid." Everyone laughs. "I'm insanely nervous, but you've all sung, so why the hell not? There are chorus parts I need help with. I'm sure you know every word like I do." The crowd cheers. "This is *Satisfied* from Hamilton."

The music starts, and a man stands and addresses the crowd. "All right, all right...."

I move to stop him, but Ms. Damia stops me and whispers, "It's the first line of the song." I squeeze their hand and head back to my seat. The man fills in the Alexander Hamilton parts of the song. And the crowd sings everything else.

Her voice bursts forward, and she's entirely on beat with the rap section. I'm not that familiar with the show. I saw it. Who didn't? But something is haunting about Ingrid singing, 'she will never be satisfied.' She's so close to something that's only hers. She's brilliant and amazing. Fuck, I'm underwater, and she's my oxygen.

The room goes nuts as she finishes the last note, holding it beyond the music. Perfect pitch and tone. She could have been a singer. She could have been anything. I'm just glad she's mine.

Chapter 18
Ingrid

Ian's been in LA for two days. I've been so spoiled. He's been all mine for three months. Lately, his music has been super bluesy, so I snuck him into the blues club Kingston Mines last week. I watched from afar as he played with some of the best. He was magnificent. They're all brilliant musicians doing what they love for the sake of loving it. No press or IG stories are being captured. They just play because it's in their soul. That's my favorite part of music—when the artist can't help but do anything but play.

I'm heading to the studio to grab my phone I left there yesterday. We Facetimed last night on my iPad. I'm ok, but I'm not alright. I miss him more than I should. I'm in too deep to get out, I think. I told my dad I met someone. He pressed for information, but I knew Sam had already filled him in.

There's a crowd in front of the studio and I head around the block to enter through the back door. I hope I don't disturb anyone's recording. It must be someone super famous to draw this kind of crowd in this neighborhood. I see Morgan but no one's recording.

"Shit. How the hell did you get by those assholes?" She asks me.

"Alley. Who's coming in? What's this about?" I rub my hands together like I'm about to find out about someone fantastic.

Morgan pops up, starts arranging carts and files, and then looks at me as if I've got food in my teeth.

"Girl, how are you this clueless? You. It's your shit-storm. They're looking for Ian and Ingrid. You're trending."

My body is numb, and I'm hoping not to throw up. This can't be happening. "No. No one knows." I shake my head, and Morgan hands me her phone.

I slide through a series of pictures. It's the two of us at the blues club on opposite sides of the room. There's one of us on the street, the distance between us, but clearly in front of Meg's house. Shit. Oh god. There's one of us kissing at the karaoke club. That's killing me that someone felt the need to expose us.

Assholes. I hope they use the money wisely. Shit. Everything is crumbling. I plug in my phone, and it doesn't stop notifying me for a full minute. I scan for only one name.

Morgan's eating a giant sandwich, and it's all over her face. "Hey, girly, you're also trending on Spotify. It's a fucking good song. I'm proud of you, baby savant."

"What the hell are you talking about?"

I pull up my Spotify, and *True in the Moment* is today's number one streamed song. He gave me credit for the song. Holy shit. Why didn't he tell me? I scroll Twitter, something I avoid like the plague. And find our hashtag: #ingridian. Not very original, but I start to read the thread. Most of it is what I expected. Gold digger or pretty boy snags a party girl. Hateful but useless. And then there's a thread about the song. There's lots of shit about him giving the party girl a job and how I fucked him for a song credit. Tears flood my eyes. My phone rings, and it's him.

I pick it up but don't know what to say.

"Wildflower, speak to me. Ingrid." My breath hitches. "Oh, sweet, beautiful Ingrid. Ignore all of that. Focus on your song being a hit and me. Don't."

"I told you. I told you this would happen if people knew and you didn't listen. You thought you were popular enough to stop it. It's ruined. I'll never be taken seriously. I've exposed Jake and Meg's house. It's all destroyed. They think you gave me the job. I'm a joke. I'm once again in someone else's shadow. I can't, Ian. I can't go back to being a brand, a nothing. I can't be with you." My words are punctuated with sobs. Morgan rubs my back. I hang up on him as my phone drops to the ground.

"Oh god. What do I do?"

Morgan pulls me to her, and I unleash the melodramatic beast. I sob until I can't anymore. My brain repeats, "Your career is gone." I don't see a way out. I have to break my heart. I can't be his arm candy. And I'm not sure I can be without him. I can't be in his shadow and never accomplish my goals. Everything I ever do will always be because I'm with him. Or my father's daughter. Or vapid Instagram girl. Or Bax's little sister or in the shadow of the 5 and their hip winery, Prohibition. It's hopeless.

I sit up finally. Morgan says, "Let me take you back to Jakes's."

"Why are you being so nice to me?"

She pulls at the hem of her Cramps t-shirt and rearranges some discarded papers.

"Look, there's very few women in this career who seek

out this kind of work, and fewer have your fucking ear. Be sad then regroup. You said your dream was to build a studio. Nobody's stopping you from doing that. Fuck em. And if no one wants to record with you, I'll threaten some people. I'll share the boys for an album. They'd line up behind you and record with you every time."

I throw my arms around her.

* * * *

IAN: It's not ruined. Everything can be fixed. I've been on the receiving end of the worst, and I still have a career. I believe in you.

IAN: Don't panic. Focus on how I feel about you and how utterly good-looking I am.

IAN: Please think about how amazing we are together. And how utterly good-looking you are. Is that better?

IAN: Your first produced song hit number one in the course of a day. And it's one of the best songs I've ever recorded. I should have told you it was being released. Sorry. I was just so excited. I wanted to do something special for you.

IAN: Talk to me, Wildflower. Talk to me, my perfect girl. Don't go dark. I'm jumping a jet to get to you. I'm coming for you, and I don't care who takes my picture. Talk to me.

INGRID: I'm ok.

IAN: Then I worried about nothing. See. Things are rosy and bright.

INGRID: Talk later.

IAN: Well, that was reassuring. Call me back, please.

Chapter 19
Ian

Not the first time I've raced across the country for love, but it's the most important. I do mean love. I should have told her. It's right there in front of our damn faces. I released the single, thinking I needed a sweepingly romantic moment to be worthy of telling her. But it backfired a touch. Fuck. Ingrid is all the music I could ever want to write. I have to fix this.

I didn't like being away from her when she worked but being in LA for two days was sheer torture. What if she made pancakes and no one ate them? I want to eat all of her pancakes. Twitter is a cruel bitch right now. I've been instructed not to Tweet. My fingers are itching to come back at people, but I know better than to start a war.

I summon the flight attendant, whose blouse mysteriously keeps getting unbuttoned. I could care less. There's only her. She's it for me, and I need her to believe that too. Fuck. Ingrid is so strong, but I want to protect her. I can't believe releasing the song was the dumbest move of my life. I thought it was a grand gesture better than candy and flowers. Shit.

"Can I get a Stella, and is it possible for me toFacetime?"

"Sure, just log on to the cabin Wi-Fi. The password for this flight is 'Dreamy.'" She scampers for the beer, then lingers too long when she hands it to me. Her fingers brushed mine. It's more annoying than anything. My mind, heart and cock have zero interest in this scantily clad woman. I head back to the bedroom to keep calling until Ingrid picks up.

I'm on call number seven when she finally answers. Her eyes are red, and my heart sinks. Her forced smile fills the screen. Her hair is on her head in a messy bun, wisps framing her delicate cheekbones.

"You're so gorgeous. I miss you so much."

She smiles but doesn't mean it. "Hi. Where are you?"

"Bedroom on the plane."

Her eyebrows raise. "That's a thing?"

"Oh, it's so much of a thing I'm going to need to show you someday. I'm going to—"

She puts her hands up. I stop talking.

"Please stop. This is too hard. I can't do this." Tears stream down her face, and I'm in physical pain that I can't hold her.

"Ingrid. Whatever you think you're doing, you need to stop. This is not the time to decide destiny for both of us. I'm sorry I didn't tell you about the single." And then I realize there's a fate worse than her crying. She's becoming the flip side of her wildflower. Her face is steel and pain. I don't want any part of this; I want the wild beauty back.

She says, and I brace for it. "Listen. You're not quite understanding. My life, the one I thought I could have, career, partner, and respect. All gone. All fucking gone. I know you didn't mean it, but you've ruined me."

This is like sitting on hot glass. That makes no sense,

but I'm pretty sure it would be as fucking painful as this. What is even happening?

"Hey, are you sure you're not exaggerating? We can figure out how to be together. This is a blip that will blow over the next time Miley has a nip slip. Calm down."

The words leaving my mouth are a bit like a car accident. I can see it coming. I know I shouldn't say it, yet my dumbass mouth let it fly. If someone told me to calm down, I'd launch on them. Turns out it's a universal thing.

She stands, and I can see boxes. What the fuck does she think she's doing?

"Are you running? Are you leaving?" She moves to a different part of the room, and her face fills the frame. Shit. I fucked up. She's no longer crying. She's just angry.

"You can date me, and your integrity is restored. That whore cheated on, wrote a book, but look how he bounces back with hot influencer Ingrid Schroeder."

"What are you saying?"

"I'm paraphrasing everyone from the Twitterverse to memes to Jimmy Fallon."

"Don't listen to Fallon. It only matters what we say." I stand and walk around a little. This can't be happening. She's not the villain or the fool. I don't understand.

Her voice is solid and true, and it scares the shit out of me.

"Ian, I've ended up taking the hit on this. I'm the vapid girl who gets a career handed to her. Troubled influencer finds a sugar daddy. I had to fight for a year to prove Dior was a job I earned. But they still reported it was handed to me. They're saying shit like, 'Paris was a bust. On to the next career.' They said I'm trying someone on. A new personality because the old one was tired."

"But you didn't and you can prove that."

"STOP! Here's the summary. You win, and I lose. And I can't have that. I'm rapidly falling in love with you, but I can't sacrifice my entire being to be with you."

She's stopped moving around, and I'm holding onto the idea she's falling in love with me. I caress the edges of my phone, wishing I was there.

"I'm always the little sister, daddy's girl, the dilettante, the wine princess. I'm Lohan, or a Kardashian. Who, by the way, have worked their asses off to be treated fairly, and it's still not happening for them. The respect they so richly deserve is held just out of reach, blinded by a red carpet or the search for the next scandal.

I know Kylie the best. I'll use my sweet friend as an example. She started her own makeup line, modeled her ass off, and created multiple dazzling capsule collections. All anyone ever asks is, "Who's her baby daddy."

"You're not them." My voice vibrates. I'm so angry at all of this. All that's slipping through my fingers while I'm on a fucking plane.

She says, "I am. And I'd be lucky to be them. But what sucks is I'm not exactly them because they're probably going to find their way out to the other side. I won't have that chance. Women are always their worst day in the press. And men, well, they get redemption and another chance. And famous men, shit, Ian, you could probably get away with anything. And me, I can't even get away with being really fucking good at my job and having a talented boyfriend. End of the day, I'm the girl who tried to steal Justin and used Daddy's winery money for attention. I'm the one who rode her model friend's coattails and scammed a job at Dior. That's my resume. Yours says, Grammy winner."

"I'm sorry it's like this. I hear you. I see you. I'll even

113

shut my mouth because I can't imagine what this is like. I'll pick up takeout on my way to the carriage house, and we can come up with a plan. I'll get my PR on it, or I don't know, but I do know I need to see you. We can fix this."

"You can't fix this." Her face is back to the vulnerable one. Tears fill her eyes. "Goodbye, Ian."

Before she can hang up, the only word I can get out is, "No."

Chapter 20
Ingrid

I throw my phone across the room. It rings, but it's not him. It's my brother's ringtone, some random Barry Manilow song he put on there. If I don't answer, my father will freak out. Dammit. This is so painful. I can't believe I have to go through this. If only he didn't put my name on the song. I don't care. I'm a producer, engineer and mix master. I'm good at it, but it's a thankless job most of the time. The joy comes in the creation. Ironically, it was his ego that he put my name on the song. He didn't know it wouldn't matter to me.

I throw a tape roll across the room. I'm building that fucking studio and hope he's still there after I figure this out. I deserve both, but I can't have them right now. I have to choose myself, even if it's ripping me in half to not be with him.

The song, *Daybreak*, squeals from my phone again.

"I'm fine." I toss stuff into a box.

"Oh, such the slinger of bullshit. You're not fine. Who do I get to kill?"

"Tab?

"Yeah. And I will rip his fucking balls off if---"

I hear her screaming, "I'm not done," in the background as my brother has clearly ripped the phone away from my insane sister-in-law. I'm headed to a hotel. I can't stay at Meg's with the press outside on her sidewalk.

"Ingrid. This isn't like you." Bax chastises me.

I sit down and play with some leftover crepes. I fold and stretch them. I take a small piece and put it on my tongue while my brother talks at me. Still tastes good cold. My heart has a hole in it. I might want him more than I want things for myself.

Maybe we could reinvent ourselves. Change our names and head to the Oregon coast. Tabi always says Oregon can fix things. We could open a small club and have local acts perform.

"LB, you're not listening. Don't make me put Tabi back on." I rip the crepe by accident. And then I destroy them all.

"Bax, this is all hopeless. I appreciate you, but there's nothing to be done."

"Are you in love with this pop star?"

"Dad or Sam?"

"Nat and then Sam. Sam had a lot of good to say."

"Dearest brother, I'll never be seen as anything but someone's accessory. It doesn't matter I fucking produced the shit out of that song. That I'm really good at this. I love it so much. I'm a punchline."

He pauses and clears his throat. "I know a bit about being thrown under the bus and being a punchline. You're the one who told me to get my shit together. So, I'm returning the favor, but first—drive."

"What?" I throw the crepe pieces in the sink and pull

my favorite travel mug out of the cabinet. I toss it across the room into a box.

"Drive. Be with yourself, and you'll figure it out. Don't hide. Don't give them the satisfaction of taking things away from you. But don't go to the airport or a train. Don't go where they're looking. Come home. Regroup and attack your life from here."

Ok, I don't always hate being a little sister.

"That's the first solid piece of advice you've given me, ever." I say as I sniff back my tears.

He laughs. "You're the one who told me to relax and figure it out. To get my shit together and stop wallowing. I'm just spitting it back at you. Stop fighting against it but find strength from it. Come spend time with all of the kids running around here. Let them remind you, you're no longer the baby."

I smile. "Can you tell Dad?"

"Nope. You know that's not how Adrian works. You're his little girl. You call him. Give him a heads-up you're coming home."

"I'm not little."

"I know."

"Can I stay at your place?"

"Our rental?"

"What happened to the house this time?" I giggle at Tabi's insistence on renovating a piece of shit ancient farmhouse. It's been a nightmare. And each disaster is funnier than the last. Bax hates it but loves her.

"Flooded. All of it. Like every inch somehow. We're jammed into a one-bedroom house on the west side."

I squeeze my lips tight. "I love you, Bax."

"Love you too, Bell."

"Not Little Bell?"

"You're too old to be Little, remember? I mean you just said it like two seconds ago. Ingrid don't think, just drive."

He hangs up, and my eyes fill. Maybe I can do this. I need a plan. I need a whole new plan.

I'm going to use my money and build a studio on the fallow land in the vineyard. I asked my dad if I could buy it with my influencer blood money, but he said no. Instead, he will parcel it off and put it in my name, and I'll pay taxes on it.

I'm getting another entrance dug out, and I was thinking of maybe building a series of one-bedroom cottages. Bands could take up residence while recording. Kind of a retreat thing. I'd even supply wine for a price if they'd like. We talked and I sent him my business plan. My dad didn't hesitate to get Becca Gelbert to work on the legal stuff. She's the oldest in our collective, and because I'm the youngest, we call each other Alpha and Omega.

My dad's the only one who knows I made millions going to parties because I never spent it. I'm Daddy's girl. You always pay your bills and put half of what's left in savings. It wasn't easy, but I did it. And now I have the money to do what I want. And I might have sold some of the gifted items. There were quite a few handbags and shoes I wore only once, for a picture, then put them away.

The more I drive, the more it all makes sense. I finally want to be from somewhere. I want to be home. I'm proud of who I am. Fuck the press.

Now, if I could stop crying about Ian, I'd be fine. Without him, I can build a studio on the down low and slowly take back my opportunities. But if that fantastic man is in my life, there won't be a minute where I'm my own person. I'll always be Ian's girlfriend who can't do anything on her own.

I can't believe something as stupid as his fame will take him from me. I'm aware I'll never love anyone like I love him. Jesus, I'm melodramatic. I might as well wear black like the old Italian widows, throw myself on a picture of him, and sob. It's time to go. I need distance to think and begin to mourn.

Chapter 21
Ian

I'm drumming my fingers on the back of the seat.

"Sir, no offense, I know you're a musician and all but could you give the the percussion section a rest?" I put my hands in my lap and turn my phone over.

> MEG: She's packing and somehow has a car now. Like out of nowhere. Boom. She owns a car. I'm panicking. I can't stall her. I don't have the talent. I'll end up telling her I texted you.

> IAN: Where's she going? I'm about an hour away. Fuck. I landed, but your fucking city has the worst traffic. And I'm from LA. At least our shit's predictable. STOP her.

> MEG: It's a big car. And it's grey. Which is not my fav color for cars. She's going somewhere.

> IAN: DON'T CARE about the color or size. Meg stop her. And throw my shit in a duffle and grab my Martin guitar.

MEG: I'll try. Stop being so pushy.

IAN: I won't survive this break-up.

MEG: Drama queen.

IAN: You owe me.

She most certainly does not. I owe her so much in this life that I take every call about Pearl or how Jake is bugging her without complaint. Or updates on her mom and sister. I do it all because she's the one that made me ready for Ingrid. Granted, I didn't know there would be an Ingrid, but Meg's the one that saw me for who I am and let me be ok in my skin. Fuck. We're not fucking moving.

"Jesus, man. Is there no other route?"

He turns back to me. "You do see, we're basically parked. No one's moving. I'm not a genie."

I try and call, no answer.

MEG: I most certainly do not owe you.

IAN: You kissed Jake before you broke up with me.

MEG: And you fucked your ex-wife before I broke up with you.

IAN: Yeah. There's that. And sorry about that again. But, um, you're so smart and talented and the best mom and biggest heart and your work is the coolest and you're beautiful…

MEG: Cram it, Pretty Boy Douchebag. Fine- I'll try and stop her. And if it weren't for you, I wouldn't have believed I could have Jake.

> IAN: WHAT? You never said that to me.

> MEG: Didn't I? Must have forgotten.
> Whoops.

It's an eternity, but we start moving again. At like a snail's pace, but it's forward, and that's all I care about.

> MEG: I'm so sorry. I'm so so sorry. She hugged me and left. She won't listen. She said she had to think.

> IAN: FUCK.

I've got nowhere to be.

"Hey, man. Take your time. Nothing matters now. Pull into McDonald's. Fries on me."

"Fries are always a good idea. But I'm sure it does matter. There's always an alternative route."

* * * *

I DON'T PLAY THIS GUITAR MUCH ANYMORE. IT WAS THE ONE I wrote my entire first album on. I always felt that it only had a certain amount of magic, and I shouldn't waste it or take it for granted. I use it sparingly. Sometimes only one song per album gets written with it.

I wrote my best album, the Meg break-up album, on a different guitar, so I thought that broke the spell. But I forgot how personal music is supposed to be over the last couple of years. It slipped my damn mind to share myself. Because the more specifically I write about something personal, the more universally it connects to people.

Now I have something to say, and it's pouring out of me

so fast I can barely keep up. I need this old axe today. I know that's dumb, but it's all I have right now. I open my mouth, and the words flow through me like a river floating me home.

Follow me, and you'll see what you want to see.

Follow me, and you can pretend all that you want to be, But if you don't follow me, you'll never really know me.

My heart isn't in the pixels. It lies beating for your skin. You're the only one who can't see that all I want to do is follow you.

Lead me wherever you want. My heart is yours. Lead me towards the open water, and I'll swim to your shore.

Lead me beyond all of this so we can get to the other side, my love.

Lead me where the vines leaf and the river bends.

I'll follow you to the end.

* * * *

I SPENT THE NIGHT TRYING TO fiGURE OUT WHERE SHE WOULD GO. hy go by car? I ache to talk to her. I got a lot of people up into the night working on the only plan I could come up with to prove to her she's making a mistake by running away without me.

I offered iHeartRadio an exclusive acoustic mini-set, and they jumped at it. They set the whole thing up here in Chicago. I haven't slept while I rehearsed and wrote.

I played *Wildflower* and then our song *True in the Moment*. And followed it up with my newest song, *Follow Me*. I figured it all out last night. I want to record it with her when I find her.

The host returns to the booth with her blue index cards.

123

"That's a gorgeous song. Was it written for anyone in particular?"

Her voice goes way up at the end of her sentence. Sly. I shove some McDonald's fries into my mouth. Music and fries. That's all the joy I'll ever get if this shit doesn't work. I should probably write McDonald's a jingle and be done with it.

I smirk at her and say, "Are you fishing or asking?"

"Both."

Fuck it. I have no filter, and my mouth got us into this mess. Maybe it will get us out. "They're all for her. Every note and rhythm. And her ear, care, and talent can only improve every song I write."

"Talent? No offense." She scoffs. Seeing Ingrid's truth play out in front of me is tough. I loathe this woman and the media machine that's marginalizing Ingrid

I made this mess, but this woman is the problem. My girl isn't taking one more second of this shit.

"Damn, you aiming to offend? Yes, talent. She's a producing genius with more skill and music knowledge than almost anyone I've ever met. Grade Repeated just cut an album with her. Pearl Jam sat down with her to hash out a couple of new singles. And she's been asked to consult on Mavis' new album. I'll be lucky if she has time for mine. No offense, but perhaps you do a little more research than TMZ."

"How was I supposed to know?" I lean towards her.

"Research." I draw the word out slowly. "Isn't it part of your job? You're like the kid who copies Wiki for a paper. Twitter's not a source."

"I said I was sorry." She stares at me with pursed lips.

"No, you didn't, but I could care less for your hollow words."

I shrug and settle my guitar back on my lap.

"No matter. I'm contractually obligated to play four songs in your tiresome company. I'll wrap up with a hit. I'm aware none of this will make it to air, but it all needed to be said."

The petty woman shifts in her chair. As if my story could be distilled down to blue note cards.

I could play my first hit, the nostalgia money song, or I play something from the soul. All I want now is to write music on my own terms and with her. But this, I play for her, whether she hears it or not.

* * * *

I finish my song, and everyone's stunned. Now I'm going to say all the promo shit in one sentence, and they can cut it together. I move around the room, summon a car and toss my gear in the case.

"Hey, Jack. Start the cart recording. I'm going to get these done in one." He's a good guy. I've known him for years. He bounces from station to station. I didn't know he was here in Chicago, but the dude always has musicians' backs. I hope he's got mine and my rant makes it to air.

I clear my throat over the woman asking a notecard question. I've gotta go.

"Wow, that was so fun. Thanks for having me. Thanks so much for listening to iHeartRadio Acoustic Sessions. I'm Ian Reilly. I'm Ian Reilly, and this is Acoustic Sessions on iHeartRadio. iHeartRadio, stream it today. Hey, I'm Ian Reilly, and coming up next on iHeartRadio are three new acoustic songs and a classic. Acoustic Sessions has been brought to you by T-Mobile. This is Ian Reilly, and you're listening to iHeartRadio. Hey, it's Ian Reilly. Yo Yo Yo, it's Ian Reilly. It's Ian Reilly and I don't give a shit about the woman next to me but I've got four acoustic songs up next. Ian here and I've got four fresh acoustic songs for you coming up next on iHeartRadio Acoustic Sessions brought to you by TMobile."

I bow to the woman and reach for the exit. I glance at the engineer, and he gives me a thumbs-up as I whip the body mic off. I also love that they can't air my shit until they pay up to ASCAP since I don't own one of the songs I played.

"You can't just leave." She bristles.

"You came to this 'music' session with takedown in your eyes, darling. That's not a game I consented to play. Take your invasive cards and shove them up your ass. Ingrid Schroeder has more integrity and grit than you'll ever know. She's worked her ass off to become an expert in a male-dominated field, and she's only beginning. God forbid anyone wants to step out of the box they've been put in."

I glance back at Jack, the engineer, and he smiles. Then he says over the intercom, "And that's a wrap. Good stuff, Ian. Tell your girl if she ever wants to get into radio to look me up. If she really does have board skills."

I grin. "She does, but I think she's a producer." I bolt out the door and scramble into a car.

MEG: No word from her.

My heart falls because I thought she'd text Meg. At least tell her she's ok. My fingers go numb. Fuck. Ok. Pivot. Plan B. I'm good at insanity. I'm done waiting for my love life to work out. I may be an idiot chasing the wind, but I have to try. I love her and should have let her in on that little secret sooner. I won't let her choose something other than us.

"Pull over right here, man. Keep the full fare. I gotta run. Thanks."

I unfold my legs from the tiny-ass Nissan Uber. I take off down Michigan Avenue towards the Hancock while I google a number. He'd freak if he didn't know where she was going. It's time to meet the parent.

I blurt out my pre-rehearsed statement before they can speak. I'm kind of jacked up and nervous. It's hard to meet one of your idols. "Hello, I'm trying to reach Adrian Schroeder. Is this a good number for him?"

"It's a terrible number for him. This is Prohibition Winery, and he has his own winery. But I could take your number for his son."

"Bax." It pops out of my mouth. "Yeah. Um. I don't even know where to start with this. Who am I talking to? And do you know Ingrid Schroeder?"

"We have no comment at this time." She hangs up the phone. Shit. I call back, and she doesn't answer. I look up Schroeder Estate Vineyards and Winery.

"Schroeder Estate Winery, how may I help you?"

"Adrian Schroeder, please."

"I'm sorry, sir, your number is part of a blocked list. Have a good day." She hangs up. Shit. I was blackballed pretty fucking quick. I bust into a coffee shop and want to be recognized for the first time in my life. I walk over to a couple of women. Both of their phones are on the table.

"Hi. My name is Ian. I need a favor. I need a phone."

"Ian Reilly?" Eyes wide but smiling.

I nod. The woman slides her phone across the table, and I seize it. I take a quick selfie with the ladies, then give them the cheeseball wink. The one I used to use to pick up women. I was a clueless fuck.

I redial Prohibition.

"Prohibition Winery, this is Natalie." She sounds nicer now.

"Natalie. Hi. Let me explain, do not hang up...." And she clicks. I put down the phone and scoop up the other one. Now I've gained the attention of the rest of the coffee shop. I wave to them.

"I'm trying to find her, ok. She left because of you people."

Three patrons who were filming me put their phones down. I address them directly, even though they're only a tiny part of the issue.

"Hell yeah, you're a part of the problem, strangers in this coffee shop." There's a silence, and I need them on my side. I'm cranky as fuck, and I need to curb it.

"Now, I might need all your phones. So, nobody goes anywhere." I nod to the barista, who is taking my picture. "Anything you people want to eat or drink is on me, ok? Order it up, folks. Grab some scones for home. Clear this joint out."

A girl in the back walks up to me and offers me her phone. "You look good together. And I'm sorry I clicked on the pictures. I just wanted you to be happy after what that woman did."

I guess not all fans are jackals. I grin. I take her phone and take a selfie with her. Then I turn back to my mission.

"Prohibition Winery, this is Natalie."

"Baxter Schroeder, please. It's life or death."

"If I used crass language, this would be a good place for it. I don't know what press organization you work for but stop harassing us." Click.

I look around. "They think I'm People fucking magazine. Who's next? Give me a phone."

Another voice, a deeper feminine voice, answers, "Prohibition Winery, this is Tabi how can I make your day even better?"

I clear my throat and speak very authoritatively. "I need to speak with Baxter Schroeder."

"The fuck you will. I don't know who the hell you are, but it's in your dick's best interest to back off this line of questioning. I can do this all-fucking day long."

"Please let me explain."

"Oh my god, the balls on you. Well, sorry to tell you, mine are bigger."

I blurt out, remembering who this is and trying to prove I know her, well, of her. "Tabi! You're married to Baxter. You're the..." Click.

I move on to the next phone. She answers right away, "Not today, asshole."

"What if I was a customer?"

"Don't care." Click.

I scream. "They think I'm the freaking press! Help, anyone. I'm open to all ideas. What do you have?"

There's a girl about sixteen years old. "I have an idea." She dials and puts it on speaker.

"Prohibition Winery, this is Tabi."

"Hello, my name is Chelsea, and I have an Ian Reilly on the line for you."

"Ian Reilly? Chelsea, for real? You're not messing with me and turn out to be secretly some press snitch?"

"No ma'am. I am just Chelsea and I swear, it's just Mr. Reilly. I can send a picture if you like."

"Fine. Chelsea have a good day, I'm sorry if I offended

you. I'm just trying to protect someone. Thanks, let me talk to him."

Chelsea hands me the phone. I whisper to her, "Chels, if this works, you get tickets for life." She squeals, and her shoulders hike up to her ears. I grin and turn my attention to the phone.

"Don't hang up," I say.

Her voice explodes in laughter. "Shit, why didn't you tell us it was you?"

Chapter 22
Ingrid

"Dad." I burst into tears. "Little Bell. Are you hurt?"

"Everywhere. It hurts everywhere without him." I cry for a bit, and he's silent. I regulate my breath. "Dad."

"Oh, honey. Trust me, of anyone on the planet, I know that feeling. Every day, it still hurts that your mother died and left my cranky ass alone. Are you on your way?"

He lets me stew in it for a moment. Then, I wipe my face, so I can see the road.

"I'm on I-80 now." I sniffle.

"You know I won't sleep until you're here safely. So let me ping your phone from time to time."

"Fine." I roll my eyes even though I feel better about driving by myself if someone knows where I am.

"Tabi and Natalie had an exciting day." He pauses for dramatic effect. He likes to do that. "He called Prohibition."

"Who?" My heart just about stops. It can't be.

"Him. That's who. He was looking for me." My breath is gone. I pull into the right-hand lane and slow down a little.

"What?! What did he say?" My heart is racing and

aching. Is that a sign of love or a heart attack? Maybe they're the same thing.

"He wanted to know where you were and talk to me. Unfortunately, I was out in the blocks with your sister and missed the call."

I blurt out, "He reads your blog."

I run my hands over the steering wheel. There's no way he'll ever get over it. I ran at the first sign of trouble. Jesus. I'm not vibrant, beautiful, strong wildflowers. I'm a plain ole ratty-ass stepped-on crocus. I ran, and he's trying to follow me by reaching out to my family.

"You there? He reads my blog? At least that's one. And one is the loneliest number." My dad laughs at his dad joke.

"He read it when we were apart. He said it was the only way to get any information about me. He still reads it every morning like the newspaper."

"He's got good taste." I smile. "Where are you, Bell?"

"Not far. I couldn't really motivate. I'm going to take my time. I slept downtown last night. I'm a couple of hours outside of Chicago." I look at the next exit. "I'm in Iowa City."

"Pull off the road and pull yourself together. I don't like you driving this upset. Go ahead and get a hotel. Order in room service. Sleep in. Sleep does wonders for mild depression."

"Dad. You can't say things like that. But sleeping in and room service does sound perfect." I pause for my own dramatic effect. "I'm so sad. I miss him so desperately, but the situation is hopeless."

I pull off at the exit and search for a hotel with room service instead of a breakfast buffet.

"Bell, I say this for your own good. Nothing is hopeless. He's not dead. Pull your head out of your ass."

I laugh at my dad. We've always said everything to each other. My brother and sister were out of the house by the time I was nine. It's always been the two of us. Because I didn't know her, I missed the idea of my mom, but not her. I had my dad and the aunties and the winery families.

The milestones sometimes sting, things a mother should be attending or caring about. Her best friends did what they could, taking me for my first bra or to girl movies. But to my dad's credit, he dug right into Mommy and Me classes and binging Gilmore Girls. I think he was comforted in doing things with me that he knew my mother would have enjoyed. Rips me open a bit that Ian knew how important my father is to me. He knew that was the path to finding me.

My dad starts again, "He's a mess. And Tabi, well, Tabi hung up on him a dozen times because she's—"

"Tell me no one told him I'm coming home."

"Would that be such a bad thing? Having someone who loves you know where you are?"

"But I don't know if he loves me."

"Then unravel your drama. Who gives a shit what people say? In the face of being alone, do you really care if they think he gave you a job?"

I smirk. "Careful. I made a lot of money off of those people."

"Perhaps this is all payback for such an easy huckster job."

"EASY? Do you know what it's like to smile non-stop or wear shoes six inches tall for hours on end? The endless taping and tucking to make sure the clothes hang right. Your job is easy." I tease him right back.

He chuckles. "Easy. A simpleton can do my job. I'm going to go drop some fruit and check brix on the back

Syrah block. So, don't mind me as I head off to my easy work."

"But you love it." I grin and sit back in the seat.

"And you love him."

"Completely." I let the phone be silent for a moment as I pull into a hotel called The Graduate. I put the car in park and sit there listening to my dad listen to me.

"Bell. I love you."

"At least someone does." He laughs, and I hang up. He's right. And my father didn't call me Little Bell. Just Bell. Did they have a meeting and decide to drop the 'Little?' Perhaps the world is shifting.

Chapter 23
Ian

I haven't slept. I hate everything and everyone. The trio at her brother's winery told me they'd get her to listen to the iHeartRadio thing. They said they'd make sure, but it's not like they can force her. I want her to hear the music. They'll cut the other stuff I said, I'm sure. As long as she hears the music, she'll know what I'm saying to her. Which is 'come find me so we can go get a smoothie' or 'come find me so we start our freaking life together already.'

I'm headed to LA tomorrow. I can't stay in exile, in my exie-bestie's carriage house, licking my wounds forever. Until she resurfaces, I'll have to wait her out.

I miss the small things. Sex is the best there will ever be, but it's how she holds a spoon or wipes down the sink after she brushes her teeth with a special towel. I don't want anyone else in the fucking world to know she flips her pillow over when she's about to fall asleep. That's all mine from now on.

She's delusional if she thinks I'm not going to chase her. I'll hold her until she's reminded that fate put us in the damn Paris closet. I'm a sappy boy now, or maybe I always have been. But I only want to be sappy with her for the rest of my life. I'm not afraid she's the one anymore. I'm not scared of diving in head first or worrying I've made another mistake. The panic is gone, and only Ingrid remains.

Here's what I'll do. I'll find her, woo her back and then stay. I don't need more money. I'll make music for the locals in the park. I'll busk on the mean Sonoma streets. I don't have a choice about making music, it's who I am, but I do have a choice about the fucking fame. If I'm gone long enough, my name will only surface in those 'Whatever happened to that poor schlub' segments on weekend editions of ET.

I'll be Mr. Mom to our kids. I don't want anything to take me from her side, and I don't want anything to take away from her work.

Fuck. I scrub my hands through my wet hair and pull-on clothes. I don't care about anything. My shit's all packed up but not very well. Meg shoved it all into random places, but I don't care enough to sort it out. And I'm afraid to ask why the bottom of one duffle is wet. I don't want to know what Meg spilled and thought she had cleaned up.

I make a cup of coffee and check the door in case there's a pancake delivery. Dumbass wishful thinking. Where the fuck did she drive?

Bax surely would have said something if she landed home, and they wouldn't have agreed to this nutty plan. I hope it works.

The cream swirls as I open my iPad to the "morning paper." I expect nothing, but I need to know how the Chardonnay pressing went. I'm invested at this point.

The vines always have a way of coming back. Finding their way home. No matter what Little Bells and whistles you try and figure out to coax them home, they find it on their own. So, if you've lost something, you might be able to catch it on 80 before it finds its way. Perhaps if you hurry, you can catch some outside of Iowa City, where we're welcoming some new distributors. The Zinfandel blend is unique and very special and has been called 'One Perfect Thing.' That's a phrase coined by my best friend about his wife. If this Zin is your 'One Perfect Thing,' then you can't be without it. I'm honored you're reading and look forward to meeting you here at Schroeder Estate Winery and Vineyards. And while you're here, perhaps you can chat with the folks at Prohibition Winery. I know my daughter-in-law is itching to make everything hospitable for you.

Holy shit. What did I just read? Is he talking to me? Is this a message on how to fucking find her? Ok. Shit. I bolt down out of the carriage house.

The back door slams behind me. Pearl runs up, and I settle her on my hip. "Pearly girly. Where's your mama?"

Jake enters. "Work. What's up?"

I quickly explain the blog and hope he can help me. He smirks at me and pushes his big black glasses up his nose. "That's amazing. Ok, let's see."

"Little Bells is a reference to her. Her family calls her Little Bell."

Jake points to the article. "I'm from Iowa. Interstate 80 goes right through Iowa City, and if you stay on it, you end up on the other coast."

I put Pearl on the counter, and her dad puts a hand on her while I pull up maps. "Holy shit. She's driving home. 80 ends right near Sonoma."

He picks up Pearl, who reaches for his glasses. He smiles. "And the rest of it sounds like you got her father's permission to pursue his daughter—literally across the country."

Jake grabs a sippy cup and fills it with water. He hands it to Pearl, and I stare at him. My heart bursts open and warms. I want that. I want a tiny Ingrid in my arms while I prepare to write music for the day. I'm staring at them and smiling. Jake interrupts my thought process.

"Shouldn't you be getting on the road?"

"Man. I can't thank you enough for all of this. For being cool with Meg being friends and the studio and…." I throw my arms around him, and he's stiff for a moment and then slaps my back.

"Hey, if she makes you even a sliver of how happy Meg makes me, you're wasting time talking to me. You're welcome. You're still a douchebag, but you're a douchebag with a good heart. And some killer blues riffs. I heard the demos. You should go in that direction. Ditch the pure pop shit. You've got some pain in there that needs to come out. And if you don't record with her, come on back. Morgan will take care of you." I kiss his cheek and Pearl's nose.

"Tell Meg I'll call her."

I shake his hand, and the door slams in my wake as I focus on trying to rent a car.

Chapter 24
Ingrid

The world is brighter and clearer now. It's all full of life and sunshine at noon. I had an excellent breakfast and grabbed a chicken salad sandwich for the road. I'm going to get to Sonoma and ask him to visit, and we'll see how it goes. No one gawked at me here or wanted to take a selfie with me. Perhaps there's life outside the spotlight. I've been in hiding for too long.

The machine is still churning, though. His single is being lauded, but not because I had anything to do with it. They keep asking, "Who really did the work?"

Morgan went turbo for me and posted all she could to her small cult. I adore her, but the machine is too big to be the ghost in it for me.

Ian keeps texting. I'm saving them up to read all together like a novella of sadness. I swing onto the highway just after one. I'm listening to only NPR and podcasts. I need to be without music for a minute.

An hour in, my phone pings a reminder that I didn't set. It echoes through the car that I did not pair it with. My sister's wife must have hacked my phone. She does that for a living. They call her a white-hat hacker, hacking for good, not evil. We've all gotten used to knowing Mel is watching. She mostly sends me funny little messages through all kinds of electronics. She helped me hide when I went to France by catching pictures of me before they went viral.

My phone speaks, "Turn Your Radio On." I didn't opt for satellite radio, but it pops on, and iHeartRadio blares into my new SUV. My phone goes silent when the radio tunes in. Mel is scary good.

His voice throws me. Apparently, my family is sending a message. I pull into the right-hand lane.

"Hey, I'm Ian Reilly, and coming up next on iHeartRadio are three new acoustic songs and a classic."

Three? He only had two completed. I'm hungry, and if I'm going to listen and torture myself, I might as well make it an event. Dust kicks up as I ease to the side of the highway. I should go to an exit, but I've decided to really dig in on the concept of desperation and sadness of eating chicken salad on the side of the road. It pairs well with listening to the love of my life singing about love, and I can't fucking have him.

The sun and cool breeze flow through the roof and windows. I leave them all open and blast the radio. I spread a blanket over the car's hood and gather my picnic. The first song is *True in the Moment*. And although it hurts, the song is really fucking good. If I allow the sadness to ebb, I can feel the pride burst from my every pore.

I sip my soda when song number two comes on. The one that's super bluesy, and I love it. I love him so much, and I wish this could be different. But more than that, I love the way he loves me. We never said it to each other. It didn't feel necessary since we both felt it. I hope he knows that. I probably should have said it.

This song is fun and dark and funky and perfect. And it's called *Wildflower*. The patter in between is annoying, and this woman is clearly trying to get some kind of scoop.

I don't know the third song. But it's beautiful. Its soul oozes into mine, and I realize it's about us, not just me.

Follow Me.

I love it so much. All of this hurts even more. It's haunting and so soulful. The producer in me is so proud of him for following a different path musically. The Ingrid in me wants to disappear into that song and live there forever.

Oh god. I shouldn't have run from him. I should have trusted we could figure it out. I was so ruined by what everyone was thinking about my work that I forgot to let it stand on its own. The song ends, and tears stream down my face. I need to talk to him. I scramble off the car and collect my things as well as myself. Maybe someone can teach me how to tune out everyone but him.

My hand is almost on the handle when I hear him yelling at this woman on the radio. He's defending me. Telling them how talented I am. I bend in half as I really cry. I threw away my one perfect thing. I hope to God I can get it back. I pull my t-shirt down and straighten up. I wipe my tears and begin to twist my hair into a bun. A car pulls over in front of me. Shit. Some asshole who thinks I'm a damsel in distress. I ignore him and pull at the door to open it.

"STEP AWAY FROM THE CAR!"

I look inside my car and then back at the voice bellowing on the side of I-80. It's him. Both of them are him. He's jogging and gets to me pretty damn fast. I turn and hit his body with too much force while an acoustic version of *Don't You Worry 'Bout A Thing* plays.

His cream skin blushes as I stroke his cheeks. His hands find their way around my waist. He smirks, and the sun highlights the gold flecks in his brown eyes.

"Are you nervous?" He pulls me close, and good tears stream down my face. His version is lovely. I can make it better, but it's still very good.

"Yes." I gasp out.

"Then we should dance."

I shake my head and then answer him. "Yes. Yes. You can have all my dances."

"I'm so sorry I'm late. And I forgot to tell you something."

"What?" I smile at him.

"I love you." Before I can catch my breath, he kisses me instantly. His lips are soft and perfect, and my body hums with a rhythm that's all ours. He loves me.

I'll never hear or create anything as beautiful as those words. Then his tongue sneaks into my mouth, and I moan around it. I hold his neck as he pulls me closer. And he sways, turning us in a circle. We're dancing and chasing each other's tongues around for a solid five minutes, and when he pulls back, he has a big dopey grin on his face.

"You're the jelly, the soundtrack, and the syrup."

"What the hell are you talking about?" I laugh.

"To my peanut butter, to my life, and to my pancakes. Wildflower, I love you so fucking fiercely even your family already knows we're written in the stars."

I shift my hands tighter around his neck. We're close. "They made me listen."

He kisses me softly. "They told me where to find you.

You really should read my 'morning paper.' It's quite illuminating." My eyes are wide as I stare at him.

"My dad?"

He kisses me softly, and I let it languish. He whispers, "Your dad. Among others."

I grin and say, "They're a feral bunch. This plan has Sam written all over it. I'm sure Bax wouldn't listen to Natalie, but Sam can get anyone to bend. And he's the most romantic of all of us. Or used to be."

He kisses me again. "I don't know the specifics. My part was to race down I-80 to find the love of my life. We can fix this you know, but we can't do it if we're not together."

I breathe out slowly. I pull him closer and say, "I'm starting to understand that. And you're here. You came after me." I can't help but sigh and pull him closer to me.

"I'm not sure what you're not getting. I'd follow you anywhere."

"You'd follow me?"

"Anywhere. All platforms." I laugh, and then his face turns vulnerable. "Nothing else seems to matter at all except that. You call the shots. And I think you're going to be pretty busy. I got a text today from someone who wants to know if you have openings in your recording schedule."

My eyes go wide. "I'm sorry, what?"

"I told Ed you were booked up with my new album, but maybe you could fit him in later in the fall."

I walk away from him and kick all the dirt around me. My car's radio is still a descant over the horizon as I stare at it.

"And he wants me? Even though I don't have a studio yet. You're friend wants to record with me?"

"Yes. He wants Moment's sound, and Morgan slipped

him a couple of demo tracks from Jake's new stuff. He wants you. Not your followers." I grin uncontrollably and turn to him.

My words burst out with pure raw emotion like a shotgun. "Then we better get busy building a studio. Tell your friend, Ed, yes."

He takes me in his arms, and all the pieces of me come together to be more than I could have ever imagined.

Ian smirks and says, "Ok then. I'll let Mr. Sheeran know."

"Oh, My Fucking God." His mouth silences me as my body zings. This is all too much. Good thing I have a couple of days' drive to process all of this.

He pauses. "I love you so very much. Like forever love you."

I slide my fingers into his floppy brown hair. He grins.

"Then you should probably follow me home because I love you more."

"Hotel first, then home."

"You know this trip is thirty-one hours, and I've only managed five hours in two days."

"Cool. Let's take our time. Like a month or so?" He squeezes me into him.

A month. I could do that. It will take that long to pour the foundation and get some walls in my studio.

I kiss him. "Deal."

"Now, about that hotel?" He grinds his pelvis into me, and I laugh.

I ask, "Next exit?"

He smiles, kisses me quickly, turns me around in his arms, and pushes me toward my car. I'm still standing, stunned and laughing. I strain to hear him over the zoom of cars.

"Chop, chop, woman. We've got forever to get to. And I really need to meet your dad. He's going to need help with that tricky Merlot lot."

I grin, turn around, and race towards my car and future.

THE END

Epilogue
Later

INGRID

Ouch. Fuck. That hurts. I'm on my stomach, propped up on my elbows. The buzzing sound is actually soothing. The outline was done a month ago, and today I'm here for color and shadow. David Gelbert, one of my 'big brothers,' drew the perfect tattoo for me; wildflowers entwined around a guitar. The studio is thriving and aptly named, Wildflower.

We're adding two more one-bedroom bungalows next month. Turns out some of the bands like to come here and write before they record. It's quite the little village vibe I've created.

Ian's not toured or left my side as I produce music. Well, he follows my father around, learning all he can. Ian's obsessed with becoming a vintner. He's calling it his second and third act. He stands at my sister's side when she starts making her magic with our wine. He's also started poking around the other vineyards in the '5' to learn it all. They seem to tolerate him ok, and he truly gets on with Becca's man, Brick. Ian's making a life, playing music around town, and learning to clean the crush pad. Glad one of us likes the winery business.

The bell over the door dings, and he's instantly down on one knee. His sexy brown eyes, dancing and earnest, take my breath every time he looks at me. His hair is cropped a little closer to his head now, but I fucking love him so very much. He shoves something toward my face, and everyone around the shop gasps. He flips the top, and there's an enormous sapphire ring. It's surrounded by small diamonds, ala Princess Diana's ring. The buzzing on my lower leg stops.

"Ingrid Sarah Schroeder, you're my entire world. I love you. Will you marry me?" As I roll my eyes at him, there's heightened tension in the air.

"Nope. And you have got to stop asking."

He snaps it shut and pulls a chair over. He sits backward on it and kisses me. The buzzing continues, and I wince.

He says, "You can take the slight pain there, dream-killer. Are you ever going to say yes?" His lips curl into a smile that sets all of me on edge and in need of relief. So damn hot.

I say, "Eventually. But not yet. The rings are getting prettier, though."

He grins widely. "What should we do with this one?"

"How about you return it?" He shoves the ring back into his tight jeans pocket.

"Is it the ring or the proposals you have a problem with?" He grins at me, and I want this tattoo business to be done so we can retreat to our relatively modest home up on Lovell Valley Road. It's a three-bedroom California bungalow, and it's perfect for us. Just enough distance from everyone but still overlooking vines and the valley. It feels new to me after a lifetime of living under other people's roofs.

The studio, which sits at the back of my Dad's property, has its own road and entrance. It also has a never-ending supply of wine. There's a mostly glass room off the back where the windows overlook the grapes and hills my family's winery sits at the base of. That's the room Ian wanted for himself. I never let other musicians use it. It's his sacred space, and he goes there all the time.

We've produced and released an album and five songs together, and when he won record of the year last year, he asked me to accept for the two of us. A spotlight I made for myself and was thrilled to step into.

He started asking me to marry him the very first month we got to Sonoma. We have time. But it doesn't stop him from asking me frequently. Sometimes the proposals are elaborate, and some seem spur of the moment, like today. It's getting harder and harder to say no—I think that's his plan.

He kisses me again, and his lips still breathe life into every cell of my body. "Maybe I'll ask you," I say on his lips.

"It's more fun asking you repeatedly. Wait until you see the next ring."

"Everything's more fun with you." I wince again. "Except getting a tattoo."

"I love you, Wildflower."

"I love you too. You're my favorite person. How could I not love you? Everyone loves Ian Reilly."

"Come on, marry me." He pleads.

I shake my head, and he sits back down. "Why do you want to marry me so badly?"

He puts his hands behind his head and says, "I want to be in Adrian's will. Duh. That's a pretty sweet piece of property you're set to inherit. I'd be a fool to let you slip away on a technicality."

I laugh hard, just like I do every day with him. I flinch again as laughing shakes my body. Much to the chagrin of my tattoo guy, who forces my leg back into position. I rest my head on my forearms and stare at my forever.

In a dreamier voice than I intend, I say, "You can have it all as long as I get you."

"Is that a yes?"

"Not yet. But soon."

"I'll take it." He leans the chair towards me, kisses me one more time, then hops up.

"Where are you going?"

"I've got a ring to return and another one to buy. And the aunties want a word with me about a ritual or some shit. Be back later."

I grin as he waves to me through the window. And now I know exactly when I'll say yes. Once the five families get involved, everyone is helpless against them and their tide of love. He'll see.

The end.

* * * *

THANKS SO MUCH FOR READING THE FIRST OF THE CARRIAGE House Chronicles. There will be three more randomly released this year, and if you pre-order, they'll just appear on your Kindles! The next one is and enemies to lovers novella called _Sound Off_. Maybe a spring release? Who knows? Pre-order here —> https://mybook.to/ SoundOffCarriageHouse

And my newest release where you can get another

glimpse of Ian & Ingrid is **Residual Sugar Gelbert Family Winery.** It's time the Alpha got her story.

And if you need more Meg & Jake & Ian

(Here's their original story)

Shock Mount and Crossfade.

More Meg & Jake

Present Tense, a ChiTown Stories spin-off -Jillien & Liam's second chance

More Ingrid & 5 Families - check the next page for all the info.

My website has reading orders and a family tree, so you can follow along as the universe expands.

You can also join my newsletter and get all the information about the Chronicles or upcoming releases there! And you don't want to miss out on the button I can't figure out how to delete from my newsletter.

www.kellykayromance.com

Feel free to drop a review at Goodreads, Amazon or Bookbub.

Reviews are the lifeblood of the indie author, and I'm so incredibly grateful for every rating, word and reader. Thanks so much. Let's do it again soon.

Xo

Kelly K

Hey Kel, what else can I read?

I'm so glad you asked.

Five Families Vineyard Romances
Interconnected standalone series exploring the lives and loves of five winery families.

LaChappelle/Whittier Vineyard Trilogy (Josh & Elle)
Crushing, Rootstock & Uncorked

Stafýlia Cellars Duet (Tabi & Bax)
Over A Barrel & Under The Bus

Gelbert Family Winery
Meritage: An Unexpected Blend (Nat & David)
Residual Sugar (Becca & Brick)

STIL TO COME
Pietro Family
Pre-order is live
Langerford Cellars

Hey Kel, what else can I read?

* * * *

CROSSTOWN BOSTON CREW: A SECOND CHANCE SERIES

Keep Paris
enemies to lovers, workplace romance with a second chance French twist
Keep Vegas
Coming 2023 - Pre-order is live billionaire, different worlds, second chance, reverse grumpy sunshine

Standalone

Side Piece: A workaholic romance
An instalove, workaholics romance about cheating on their jobs not each other.

Holiday Disasters
(with Evie Alexander)
A completely bonkers rom com novella series focusing on one trope and one holiday at a time. They're two side by side interconnected novellas.

EVIE & KELLY'S HOLIDAY DISASTERS

<u>**VOLUME ONE**</u>
Cupid Calamity
Cookout Carnage
Christmas Chaos

CARRIAGE HOUSE CONTEMPORARY CHRONICLES

Funny, steamy, smart novellas for when you don't know what to read next. All set in the same Chicago Carriage House. And all a part of the CHI TOWN STORIES universe. Released randomly throughout the year! You can pre order them and they just appear when I've finished them. Like a surprise for your Kindle.

Follow Me - Out now: second chance, forced proximity, rock star

Sound Off: Musical enemies to lovers

Something Good: Age Gap, Nanny, Rockstar
This story will first appear in Twisted Tropes Anthology out on March 30

For the Rest of Us - See if they an find a Festivus miracle.
Holiday, M/M, Marriage in crisis, One Bed

Acknowledgments

Quick thank yous!

Tori Alvarez. My friend, thank you for inspiring this story in the first place with your fabulous anthology title: A Series of Unfortunate Meet Cutes. I'll never look at supply closets the same.

My Shock Mount and Crossfade editor, Erin Young, who helped me bring Ian, Meg and Jake to the world

Aimee Walker for editing this piece and loving Ian so much that she was joyous that I brought him back.

Julia Jarrett who said, what story do you feel is unfinished in your own universe. Thank you.

My sister Allison and friend Cindy who have known Ian almost as long as I have. They're OG Meg fans. Thanks for so many years of support.

St. Augustine, FL. - - It was when I lived there I began to think about what I wanted my life to look like. Happy to say I'm getting closer.

I wasn't sure I knew what I was doing, but when I sat down to write my very first book, Meg, Jake and Ian popped into my head, almost fully formed. I'm proud to say they're still kind of the same. If you will, they're my security blanket, and I'm thrilled to tell the rest of The Committee's stories in the upcoming Carriage House Chronicles. Those characters always felt a bit undone.

Thank you to the kid and husband for just about everything else.

Readers, bloggers, friends. Thank you for being here and jumping down this rabbit hole with me.

Up next is Wade Howell and Morgan Sumner's tale. They don't like each other a whole lot, but at some point, the story they're both trying to tell flips them upside down. It should be along this spring or so.

About Kelly Kay

Kelly Kay is the author of twelve funny, smart, steamy, full-length contemporary romances. She's also the co-author of the wildly popular novella series Holiday Disasters with author Evie Alexander. She's the wife of a writer and mother of an eleven-year dynamo of a boy and is currently a little sleepy. There's a good chance she's either holding a cup of coffee or a glass of wine right now.

She cleverly figured a way to drink wine and write simultaneously by creating her popular small-town series, Five Families Vineyard Romances, which are set in the California wine country. Her books are currently available on Amazon and free in Kindle Unlimited.

Random good things in the world: pepperoni pizza, Flair pens*, road trips, coffee, sidesplitting laughing fits, matinees on a weekday, the Chicago Cubs, a fresh new notebook full of possibilities, bourbon on a cold night, Fantasy Football, gaggles of friends, witty men, local zoo in the rain and that moment when a character clicks in and begins to write their own adventure.

Oh, and wine. I she likes wine. (duh)

*purple Flair pens rule
Feel Free to Follow Kelly in the following places!
Or you can join the newsletter here
https://www.kellykayromance.com/

All writing/book playlists can be found on Spotify!
Spotify: http://bit.ly/KellyKayPlaylists

Made in the USA
Monee, IL
17 April 2024

57086471R00095